THE FACELESS MAN

An absolutely gripping crime mystery with a massive twist

Detectives Lennox & Wilde Thrillers Book 2

HELEN H. DURRANT

First published in Great Britain 2021
Joffe Books, London
www.joffebooks.com

ISBN: 978-1-78931-716-9

*For Imogen and Stephen, hope you will both
be very happy in your new home.*

PROLOGUE

The warning was clear enough. It was just a pity Dean had chosen to ignore it — he was young, intelligent, and had a promising future. But the interference had to stop. He was getting too close. Bottom line, Dean was a danger to his enterprise, and he had to go.

The arranged meeting place was the kids' playground in the park. At night, apart from the lights by the entrance, the place was pitch black, deserted. Besides the drumming rain, the only other sound was the swings squeaking in the strengthening breeze, their dark shapes adding to the eerie atmosphere. The man shivered and turned up his collar. It was a miserable night. Shame about Dean. This wasn't how he wanted it to be, but the lad had sealed his own fate by refusing to keep out of his business.

The man smiled to himself. Dean had wrongly imagined that approaching from behind gave him the advantage of surprise. He had failed to realise that the man couldn't have survived in this business by being sloppy.

"Why here?" Dean asked. "There's a pub across the road — drier and more comfortable."

"Too busy. I don't want to be seen with you, so this place is better."

A candid reply, but the lad didn't pick up on its significance. Neither did he remark on how the man was dressed, in motorbike leathers, tight-fitting gloves and with a rucksack on his back. "Let's walk."

"This isn't going to be a job offer, is it? Only there's no way I could work with you."

The man laughed. Now where had the lad got that idea from? "Not what I have in mind at all."

"Where are we going?"

"Nowhere in particular. A wander round, have a chat and get some exercise. I've not been to this place in a while. Is the boating lake still here?"

"Yeah. But I don't like water," Dean admitted. "Never learned to swim, see."

The man knew that too.

They stood silently at the lake's edge, looking out over the watery expanse, listening to the boats knocking against each other and the click of the masts.

After some time, the man broke the silence. "You've stuck your nose into my business once too often, Dean. It can't continue. You do know that, don't you?"

The lad stepped back from the water lapping at his trainers. "I know the truth — what you are, what you do. I should go to the police again, try and speak to them."

"You know I can't allow that."

"Huh. You can't stop me," Dean scoffed.

The man laughed. Dean wasn't seeing the bigger picture.

"Do you have any evidence of what I do? You don't, do you?" Though he had no idea what real information the lad had on him, or how long he'd been keeping tabs on his activities.

"I might have," Dean said. "Sort you out good and proper that would. Make the job easier for the police too." He tapped his head. "In any case, I have no intention of telling you what I've got. But know this. I hold all the aces."

The man weighed up the risks. If Dean did have anything, it was unlikely to be much. The man was meticulous in ensuring he left no evidence for others to find. But would the law continue to dismiss Dean's tale as simply the ramblings of an over-imaginative teenager?

Dean laughed. "And I know the username you look for on that website. You're not the only one who lives in the shadows, you know."

The man was curious. "Okay, what else d'you know about me, Dean?"

The lad grinned. "I'm not saying anything else."

"Have you told anyone?"

"No, and I won't if you agree to my terms. Pay me," the lad demanded. "You must earn a packet, so pay me to stay quiet."

The man looked at Dean's face. He meant it. The lad was serious. He nodded, as if he were weighing this up. "It might work. But I have a far better idea."

"I'm all ears."

Dean was still wearing that self-satisfied expression when the thin blade slid effortlessly between his ribs. The man had positioned it at a slight upward angle on the left side of his chest. It went straight into his heart.

With a low groan, Dean Greenwood fell to the ground. Game over.

The man fished around in Dean's pockets and removed his mobile, wallet, and house keys. No way was he making this easy for the police. It was time to tidy up. He hoisted the lad up and laid him in the nearest boat. Taking the petrol can from his rucksack, he emptied the liquid over the body. He lit a match, flicked it between his finger and thumb and gave the boat a hefty shove with his boot. It floated out into the centre of the lake where it exploded in a ball of flames. That would put paid to Dean's meddling and any stray DNA.

CHAPTER ONE

Day One

"Where've you been?" DS Jess Wilde hissed. "The call came in over an hour ago. I've been standing here in the cold so long I've lost all feeling in my feet."

DI Harry Lennox glanced down. No way, not in those winter-weight jobs. As well as a heavy coat, Jess was wearing leather boots with lace up fronts and a flurry of fur around the top. "Sorry. I was driving back. With all the traffic on the motorway, you're lucky I made it at all." He looked down at the body in the boat. "I was told this was an accident. Down to kids fooling about by the lake. This is way more than that."

"Driving back from where?"

Here we go. Why did Jess have to question his every move? "Scotland," he said. She looked surprised. "I paid a flying visit home, had to get a few things straightened out. And that's all you're getting. A guy has to have his secrets."

"Well, you've certainly no shortage of those, Harry Lennox."

Tricky subject, time to change tack. "Given this wasn't an accident, have we got anything else apart from the body?"

"Not yet. The killer left no obvious clues."

"Who found him?" Harry asked.

"A dog walker, out first thing. He saw the boat bobbing about unmoored and dragged it up to the edge of the lake," Jess said. "When he rang it in, he suggested that the death could be due to a fight that got out of hand. Cheetham Park has its fair share of trouble, at night the place is often full of kids messing about."

"What do you make of that?"

"Not a theory I'd go with. This looks deliberate. Whoever did it even tried to burn the body, probably to destroy evidence." She nodded at the boat. "We need the PM results for confirmation but it looks like a stabbing. There's been a lot of rain and there is still what looks like dried blood on the floor of that boat."

Harry sighed. So much for the quiet life. "We need to find out who he was."

"He's a kid, it's early, not yet eight in the morning. Chances are he's been missing from home all night. With luck his parents will have been on by now. I'll ring the station," Jess said, "get Colin to check."

Dr Melanie Clarke, the home office pathologist from the Reid Centre, was already examining the body. "Not pretty, is it? The fire was down to petrol being poured over the lad. Fortunately for identification purposes, it didn't do too much damage to his head and face. An initial flare, intense heat, and then one of those torrential downpours we had last night caused a large puddle to form at one end of the boat and his head became submerged in it."

Harry went forward for another look. "Poor sod. I hope it was quick."

"Despite the rain, this won't be an easy one. That cagoule he's wearing melted onto the body. It'll make our work all the more difficult," Melanie said.

Harry looked around at the huge expanse of parkland, empty apart from a small group of spectators behind the police tape. Several pairs of keen eyes were watching their every move, all of them hoping for a glimpse of something gruesome to gossip about. Harry shivered. Why did people find death so fascinating? And didn't they have better things to do?

Jess had followed his gaze. She nudged him. "Most of them are press. Word's got out and they're wondering if this heralds another spate of gang warfare."

"And there was me hoping for some down time after the last case."

"Murder never takes a break, Harry, you know that."

Didn't he just, but he wished it wasn't so keen to follow him around. Harry had moved to Ryebridge for two reasons — to escape his demons and live a quieter life. No such luck. The last case they'd dealt with had involved both — an old enemy and a network of people traffickers that spanned the globe.

"I wonder what brought our victim here?" Harry said.

"Meeting his mates, a date with a girl, who knows?" Jess looked around.

During the day, Cheetham Park was a pleasant open space, well used by the Ryebridge population. It was the ideal place to meet friends and hang out. There was plenty of open parkland for walking, a kiddies' play area, football pitches and the boating lake. There was a thriving sports club at one end — a lot of kids went there after school and on weekends. But nights were a different matter. Then it was no place to be alone. Last night it had been unusually wet. If the usual rough element had given it a swerve, who'd killed the lad?

"There's a camera on that building over there. It's where you buy tickets for the boats. We might get something," Jess suggested.

But Harry was only half listening. The park wasn't far from the town centre but the walk up to the park entrance was along a dark and unlit tree-lined lane. "How bad is this place at night?" he asked.

"Back that way it's quiet, there are no buildings as you approach the main entrance. But there is a camera, I'll get the footage organised. It covers the playground, might be useful. About a mile away is the small development I told you about. Remember, I'm in the process of buying one. But at the far end is the Baxendale, and you know what that means."

Didn't he just. It didn't matter where you were in Ryebridge, there was no getting away from that bloody estate. As he'd thought, this place was pretty much a no-go area after dark.

"There is some dealing goes on and the kids gather together in groups, drinking, making a noise and fighting. There've been loads of complaints down the years. Uniform do blitz the place regularly, but it's still happening," Jess said.

"I don't think it's down to a lads' fight that got nasty, this is different," he said. "It looks premeditated to me."

"You're right, Harry," Melanie said. "The lad was stabbed in the chest. The PM will tell us more."

"Wonder who he upset — some crazy bastard that's for sure. Knifed and set alight. Does that sound like kids to you?"

"So who did he upset?" wondered Jess.

"Is the lake deep?" Harry asked.

"No, these are rowing boats. Fall out and you can walk to the side," Jess told him. "I've done it myself in the past. Me and my mates used to muck about here when we were kids."

Melanie Clarke was supervising the removal of the body from the boat. "I'll get him back to the mortuary. The fire did some damage, but since his face hasn't been touched that'll make identification easier."

"Any obvious bruising?" Harry asked.

"You're asking if he's been in a fight? Difficult to judge until I get him back, but there's nothing I can see and there's no obvious grazes on his hands. We'll do the usual checks. We might get lucky, find something useful under his fingernails."

Harry took a photo of the lad's face with his mobile. It might prove handy if they found someone who knew him. "So, there we have it, Jessie. Murder. No fight, no accident. Pity. I was hoping to get a few more days off."

"How was Scotland? See your family?" she asked.

"Stop fishing, Jess," he said. "Nothing on that front has changed, and until it does what family I have left is out of bounds."

"And of course, if you did see your family, there'd be questions." Jess gave him one of her unimpressed looks. "I've still got a few myself."

CHAPTER TWO

Dr Hettie Trent, one of the forensic scientists working at the Reid and Melanie's usual working partner, came slowly towards them, her eyes on the ground.

"There are two sets of footprints," she said, looking up. "It's muddy just here. Water splashes on the bank from the lake, plus it rained heavily yesterday. One of the two wore boots, the other trainers, and both sets begin back there." She pointed to the children's playground. "I reckon two people walked to the lakeside but only one walked away — the one wearing the boots." Hettie smiled at Harry, the professional mask slipping. "Hello, stranger, long time no see. What have you been up to, apart from hiding from me?"

"It's been a bit tricky — personal stuff, you know," Harry said, looking embarrassed.

Hettie gave his arm a playful slap. "You're impossible, Harry Lennox, you really are. You've got a new girl. I've heard all about her. A paramedic who thinks you're some sort of hero."

"Oh, that. It was nothing."

"Nothing! I heard you took on a gunman and saved a woman's life."

"All in a day's work," he said, grinning. "It was that incident at Marsh's warehouse."

"I also heard that new DC of yours, Colin Vance, has given you a room in his flat," Hettie said. "Nice it is too, overlooks the canal. Has to be an improvement on that campervan."

Harry smiled. "It certainly is, and the neighbours are okay, too. We've quite the little gang going. You should join us one night for a drink. Me, Col and Hugh from next door make it to the Barge Inn most Friday nights. Hugh's single too, you'd like him."

"Stop trying to matchmake," Hettie said. "It won't work on me. But I'm pleased you're settling in, finding your feet at last. Good for you. You certainly look a lot happier."

"This Hugh," Jess nudged him. "Your new bestie, is he?"

"He's a dentist of all things, and he's okay." He turned to Hettie. "Talk us through what you think happened here."

They strolled back to the playground. "Here — see the patch where the grass is scuffed under that swing?" Hettie pointed to the ground. "Someone sat here. You can tell from the smears in the mud down there. We've swabbed the chain on the swing. It's possible the killer sat there while he waited for his victim."

"You think the lad met up with his killer and they then walked towards the lake together?" Jess asked.

Hettie nodded.

"If you're right, that suggests they'd arranged to meet, which means that the victim might have known his killer," Harry said. "A mate, perhaps?"

Harry's mobile began to ring, interrupting his train of thought. It was Colin Vance back at the station.

"We've had a hit on missing persons. A young man called Dean Greenwood didn't go home last night. He's eighteen and lives with his mother about half a mile from the park."

"And she's sure he wasn't with friends?" asked Harry.

"Seems he's not one for socialising, so his mother reckons that's unlikely. But she's rung round some lads from college and other family members just in case."

"Text me the address."

Call ended, he turned to Jess. "We need to go. Got a lead." Harry checked his phone and found the message giving the address. "We've got a possible name for the victim. It's not far away, back through the park main entrance and round to the right. I took a couple of photos with my mobile, including one of the lad's face. If this is his mum, she'll recognise him."

* * *

Dean Greenwood lived, or had lived, with his mother, Maggie, in a large red-brick semi in the upmarket Mayfold area of Ryebridge.

Harry pulled up outside. "I hate this part. It's grim and there's always tears." Telling someone that a family member was dead, especially if they'd been murdered, was one of the worst parts of the job.

Jess checked the scant information they'd been texted. "Grim or not, it's our job," she said, her eyes on the screen. "Mother and son only. I wonder what happened to the father — he's not listed as living here."

"Divorced?" Harry offered.

Jess didn't comment. "Come on, let's get this done. We need to give our victim a name."

He rang the front doorbell. A pale, harassed-looking woman answered. She had dark circles around her eyes, as if she hadn't slept.

"DI Lennox and DS Jess Wilde. Mrs Greenwood? We'd like a word. Can we come in?"

The woman's face lit up. "I'm her neighbour. Have you found him? Maggie's been in bits, this is so unlike Dean. She's through here." She led the way inside. "Dean hasn't even rung, which is odd because he's usually so considerate."

"And you are?"

"June Hardy. Me and Brian, my partner, live next door."

11

They followed June into the sitting room. A tearful woman was staring out of the back window. A tall dark-haired man stood by her side.

The red-eyed woman turned and looked at them. "You've found him? Please tell me you've found my son."

"Mrs Greenwood?" Harry asked. "I'm afraid we've found a body — this morning in the park — but we're not sure if it's Dean or not. It would help if we could see a photo of him."

Maggie Greenwood pointed to a large family portrait hanging on the wall opposite. "That's Dean on the right."

Harry checked the image on his phone and nodded at Jess. They'd found their victim.

CHAPTER THREE

"There's no easy way to say this," Harry began. "I'm very sorry, Mrs Greenwood . . . Maggie." He paused, giving her a moment to prepare herself. "We believe the body we've found is your son, Dean. My colleague and I are very sorry for your loss."

She looked from one detective to the other as the news slowly sank in. "How? I don't understand. What happened to him?"

The usual confusion and disbelief. In Harry's opinion, parents rarely knew enough about their kids' lives. Not that he was any sort of expert, he couldn't even hold down a relationship, never mind be a father. "He was found this morning lying in a boat on the lake in Cheetham Park."

Now Maggie Greenwood looked more puzzled than ever. "Are you sure it's him? Dean wouldn't go near open water, he was scared of it — never learned to swim, you see. And that park isn't safe. He wouldn't go there after dark. It's a hangout for local gangs, Dean knew that — he got enough grief from them during the day."

She stopped talking. In floods of tears, she got up and began pacing the floor while the four of them looked on helplessly. She was cut to pieces, overcome with grief. Harry understood that, but he needed her to focus, to remember what she could about the previous evening. "Do you want to sit down?" he asked tentatively.

"No! I want to know what happened to my son," she shouted. "You come here, tell me Dean's dead, but that's not good enough. What aren't you telling me? There's something else, isn't there? CID don't come knocking at the door if it's an accident." She stopped, took a breath, and then in a firm voice said, "I need to know how my son died."

June and Brian looked at each other, seemingly unsure of what to do. "Maggie, the inspector is right. It's been a shock," Brian said eventually. "You should sit down. I'll get you a brandy or something."

"And you are?" Jess asked.

"Brian Isherwood, June's partner. We live next door. We've all been friends for a while."

Maggie Greenwood finally sat down on the sofa, Brian's arm around her shoulders. "It was a bad night . . . all that rain," she sobbed. "I didn't want him to go out but he insisted, said he'd made arrangements. But why did he get into a boat? It doesn't make sense."

"Did he say what sort of arrangements? Was he meeting someone?"

"Dean never told me much. He came and went and said very little about what he was up to or who he met. Mostly, when he wasn't at uni or working, he was in his room."

"I'm afraid Dean was murdered." Harry gave the woman some time for the words to sink in.

Maggie Greenwood shook her head slowly. She looked shell-shocked. "That can't be right, I know some of the local lads didn't like him much, but not enough to kill him. They were jealous — my Dean was clever, did well at uni and didn't run with the crowd. I don't understand it, any of this. Dean never got into bother."

"Yes, he was a good lad, no trouble at all," Brian added.

Harry sat down facing Maggie. "I know this is a bad time but I need to ask you a few questions. Can you think very carefully before answering, Maggie? It's important we catch whoever did this to your son as soon as possible."

She nodded.

"How's Dean been lately?" he asked. "Did he seem worried about anything? Did he ever mention being afraid of anyone? Someone local perhaps?"

Maggie stared at Harry. "What are you saying? That Dean upset someone and was murdered as a punishment? Dean didn't mix with people like that. He was a bit obsessive over his hobbies, particularly his project for college." She looked down at her hands. "You'll see what I mean shortly. I presume you'll want to look at his room."

Harry nodded.

"Dean didn't have many friends, but those he did have were like him — well-mannered, pleasant teenagers. He wouldn't hurt a fly. He got on with everyone."

"Not quite everyone, Mrs Greenwood," Jess reminded her.

"Dean had been a bit off lately," June Hardy said. "I asked him about it when he helped me with the garden last week. He told me it was nothing, just him being paranoid."

"What did you take that to mean?" Harry asked.

"Okay. I suppose I'll have to tell you." June addressed Maggie. "Dean didn't want to worry you, but he was a bit jumpy about a man he reckoned was following him. He said this man might do him harm."

"Did he know this man?" Harry asked.

June continued to speak directly to Maggie. "I asked Dean to explain, but he wouldn't say any more than that. Told me I was better off not knowing, that the man was dangerous. He said he'd seen him before, we all had, a while ago when we were on that holiday up in the Borders." She smiled at Harry. "That's a Scottish accent you've got. Perhaps you know how beautiful it is around Galashiels. Anyway, all four of us — Maggie, Dean, Brian and I — took a lodge by the Tweed for a few days. It was a pleasant break, we even did a bit of fishing. Dean seemed to enjoy his time with us all, until those men were murdered close by. They were killed on the other side of the park from where we were staying but still, it spoiled the holiday, and it upset Dean. I tried to tell him it had nothing to do with us, and that we were quite safe, but I don't think Dean was convinced. Why would the killer follow him? Nonsense of course — I mean, Dean didn't witness anything. In the end he dropped it, but he did get angry when I said I couldn't recall the man. I did wonder if it was all in his head — not the murders, they were real enough, and we were all interviewed. Dean could be a bit fanciful at times, you see. He was always making up stories. He'd go places and come home full of it. The Galashiels trip was no different. This man he saw will have been just another fisherman staying at the park. The local police will have spoken to him like they did the rest of us."

"He did describe the man to me," Brian said. "He wanted to know if I remembered him. Dean said he'd been staying in the park, in one of the other lodges, but the description he gave was very general. Tall, dark hair, very fit and in his late thirties — could be any number of blokes. I asked Dean what had made him so memorable, and he said it was his eyes. He said they were ice blue, the coldest eyes he'd ever seen."

"See what I mean? Fanciful," Maggie said.

"Would that be the 'Borders Holiday Park?'" Jess asked, her eyes on her mobile.

"Yes, and there's something else," Brian said. "Dean told me that this man had given him an earful one day for spying on him. But nothing came of it."

"Do you have any photos of that holiday?" Harry asked them all. "If Dean was right, they might help."

Maggie looked puzzled. "You think Dean did see something and he was genuinely in danger? That this man murdered him?"

"We shall have to make more enquiries, then we'll have a better idea," Jess said. "But we'll certainly investigate."

"I have a lot of photos. Leave your details and I'll email them to you," June offered.

"You said Dean worked," Jess said. "What did he do?"

"He does a few hours a week after lectures at the Commodore Hotel in Manchester," Maggie said, using the present tense. "It's not far from the uni. The job's nothing special, just a little reception work and inputting data into the booking system."

"Did Dean have a mobile?" Jess asked.

"Yes, I bought it for him last Christmas. He'll have had it on him."

"It wasn't found," Jess said.

"It was on contract so the provider will give you the information you need," Maggie said. "I'll email you the details."

"Have you tried ringing it?" Harry asked.

"Of course. First thing I did when I woke up and realised he wasn't home, but it's not accepting calls." She burst into tears again.

"I will need you to identify your son formally, Maggie. Are you able to do that?" Harry asked.

Maggie Greenwood looked at her neighbours. "You'll both come with me?" she sobbed.

Harry got to his feet. "I'll send a car. I can arrange for a family liaison officer to look after you. They'll keep you up to date with events."

"Can I think about it?" Maggie said.

"Sure. Here's my card," Harry said. "If you remember anything that might help, give me a call." He paused. "Could we have that quick look at Dean's room before we go?"

"Okay, I'll show you up."

CHAPTER FOUR

Dean Greenwood's room was not standard fare for a teenage lad. It was exceptionally tidy for a start, but that wasn't what caught Harry and Jess's attention. Two large boards hanging on the wall facing the window opposite were covered in a tapestry of press cuttings and notes, some handwritten, some printed, presumably by Dean.

Harry and Jess stared at them, intrigued, trying to make sense of what they were looking at. The notes were pinned alongside newspaper cuttings showing different faces. One column was labelled 'dead' in capital letters across the top, and the other bore a question mark. On the 'dead' board the lad had collected virtually everything he could find on a number of murders that had taken place in the Greater Manchester area. Some had obviously been of special interest to him, and these were ringed in red felt-tip pen. Below them were photos of two men, labelled in scrawly writing.

"He's linked some — look at the red lines joining up the faces," Jess noted.

"Do you know why your son collected all these?" Harry asked Maggie.

"Yes, that's the project I mentioned. He was studying computer science at college. He spent every spare moment up here researching, making his notes. Bit odd perhaps, but that was my Dean."

"Didn't you ask about these people? You'll have seen the news, know that some of them were murdered. Didn't it strike you as strange that Dean was so fascinated by them?"

"Yes, of course it did. I thought it was morbid and I told him so. I was worried that he was becoming obsessive, but he just said I wouldn't understand."

Some of the faces on the 'dead' board were familiar. At least one — that of a young woman — had been the subject of a high-profile case in Hulme, in Manchester. But it was the other board that Harry was most interested in. On it were photos of three faces — one a young woman, a second a middle-aged man. But it was the third that drew Harry's attention. It was a silhouette of a man's head. No features, no colour, just a white shape cut out of cardboard. Harry felt a shiver slip down his back. Who was he and why hide his identity?

"A victim with no face," Jess said. "Very mysterious. I wonder why Dean was so coy about him."

Harry shook himself. "You can see he's named the ones who are already dead. The three on the question-mark board are all unnamed. They could be potential victims."

"You think the three of them — the blank, the young woman and the man — are all still on some hit list?" Jess asked.

"Possibly."

"I don't recognise the others either," Jess said. "From the cuttings it looks like they're already dead. One in Hulme, and the others around the Manchester area. These two," she tapped the board and squinted to read the words, "he's labelled 'Galashiels in Scotland.'"

"I recognise the Hulme case, that's Nadir Nasir. It was high profile and handled by Manchester Central. Dean certainly knew what he was up to." Harry pointed. The word 'Killer' printed out in huge letters was pinned across the top of both boards.

"What have we stumbled on, Harry? Like his mum says, evidence of an overactive imagination, a genuine college project or something more sinister?"

"I think this is Dean's very own incident board. He's spent time and energy compiling this little lot, and I want to know why. Each one of these killings, if that's what they are, need looking at with fresh eyes," Harry said.

They had forgotten Maggie, standing in the doorway, watching them.

Harry turned to look at a large desk in front of the window. "Liked his tech, your boy," he said. Dean seemed to have owned two laptops, a tablet and a printer. "Expensive kit, too. What did he do with it all?"

Maggie shrugged. "He spent hours up here — college work, he said. I never asked him much about it, all that technical stuff went over my head."

"We'll need to examine these back at the lab," Harry told her. "I'll send someone to pick them up." He waved a hand at the wall covered in notes. "Is there anyone else Dean would have spoken to about this . . . this project? A friend? Someone from college, or his work perhaps?"

"No. Like I told you, this was Dean's thing. I asked him about it often but always got the same answer, that it was to do with course work he was doing as part of the end of year assessment. I just left him to it."

Harry doubted it was that. The more he looked at the dozen or so names and faces on the wall, the more troubled he became. Where the Nadia Nasir case was concerned, he knew the Greater Manchester force were still investigating.

He studied the face of the young woman on the other board. Harry had seen her recently, he thought he recognised those huge, dark eyes, but where? Had Dean Greenwood been close to exposing a murderer? If he was right, if Dean had discovered the identity of this killer, had he threatened to tell the police? Was that what got him killed?

Both boards were important evidence. Everything on them would have to be checked out. Harry stood back and took several photos of the montage with his mobile.

"I know her," Jess said, pointing to the photo of the same pretty, dark-haired girl who'd drawn Harry's attention. "And Dean was right, she's not dead, so your theory about potential or next victims could be correct. These three are important. We need to find them. But this one'll be a problem. Why is he the only one with no features? What was Dean hiding?"

Harry had no answer to that. They needed to know a lot more about Dean Greenwood before any of this would make sense. "Mrs Greenwood, can I ask you to leave that wall exactly as it is. One of our CSI people will take the pictures down and bring them in."

She shrugged. "Okay, but it's just his college project. What possible use can it be?"

"I'm not sure yet, but it might be more significant than we think."

Maggie Greenwood went back downstairs, leaving them to it. "You think that wall is what got him killed, don't you?" Jess asked. "It's an odd one. What teenage lad d'you know does that sort of thing?"

"Well, the ones I usually meet are druggies or apprentice dealers. This is a new one on me."

"But we should check out all aspects before we jump to conclusions," Jess said. "For a start, we should make sure Dean hadn't upset one of the Baxendale's more unsavoury characters."

* * *

Back at the station, Harry briefed Colin Vance on what they had so far. "I want you to look closely at Dean's life," he told the newest member of his small team. "You know the drill — his friends and family, the people he worked with at that hotel." He gestured to the photos of Dean's wall which he'd had blown up, printed out and pinned to their own incident board. "We need to look into this obsession of his. My gut tells me it's at the centre of this case. Also, Col, find out if Dean had any connection to drug dealing or anything else that could have got him into trouble. I doubt it, but we should cover all bases."

Harry's eyes were drawn again to the photo of the young woman Jess had said was still alive. There were numerous red lines leading from her image to notes Dean had made of dates and places. One of these led to the victim from Hulme.

He turned to Jess. "You said you knew her. I've seen her myself too, recently," Harry said. He tapped the image. "What, I wonder, did young Dean know about her?"

Jess rolled her eyes. "Trust you to fixate on the pretty face. But you're right, you have seen her. That girl is everywhere — she's what's known in social media parlance as an 'influencer'," Jess explained.

"What d'you mean? What's one of them?"

"That is Lana Midani. Get onto any of the social media platforms and she'll be all over it. The kids love her. They copy what she wears, her make-up, the lot. She's the latest and hottest property in advertising."

Harry nodded. Now he was getting it. "Is it possible that Dean simply had a crush on her, and that's why she's on his wall? If this Lana thought anyone was watching her, spying, she'd cry blue murder. She'll have 'people' who'll look after her, keep the likes of Dean and anyone outside her circle well away."

"A crush? It's possible, I suppose, but we can't be sure, Harry. Have you seen the local rag?" Jess took a copy of the *Ryebridge Advertiser* from her desk drawer and showed him the front page. "Lana is in town, here in Ryebridge and staying at the Metropole." The Metropole was a throwback from the Edwardian era when Ryebridge was a prosperous cotton town. Back in those days, the hotel was patronised by the wealthy mill owners. "I bet Dean did know something.

Think about it. Our killer is in town too and it's possible Dean had worked out why."

Harry had to give her that one. Perhaps Dean had arranged the meeting, tackled the killer, threatened to expose him to the police, and it led to his murder. "Lana Midani is one of the three. We need to contact them all, but we'll start with her. It would help to know if the other two are local."

"They might be, but we'll have difficulty with him." Jess tapped the blank face. "The other bloke could be local. I'll run his image through the database, see what comes up. Dean got that picture from somewhere."

"He could have found it on a social media profile," Col said. "Got his name or had a suspicion and went from there."

"So, why hasn't he named these three? He's named the others, the ones we think have already been killed," Jess said.

"Probably because those three aren't dead yet," Harry chipped in. "But we can't know for sure." He looked at Colin. "Check whether this lot are victims and the status of the investigations into the deaths."

"What have we got here?" The voice coming from the rear of the room belonged to Superintendent Roderick Croft, affectionately known to the team as 'Rodders.'

"Evidence of a bloody maniac, sir," Harry said. "This is from the house of our young victim, Dean Greenwood. It's possibly the reason he was killed. He appears to have discovered a series of murders across the country. These three," Harry tapped the three with no names, "we think are possibly local and still alive."

Rodders stared at the board. "With so many victims and a list of potentials, I can't believe there isn't already an operation underway to catch this individual."

"The Hulme killing is still active, sir," Harry said. "We'll check the others."

"I'll make some enquiries myself and get back to you," Rodders said, and left them to it.

CHAPTER FIVE

Lana Midani was not a happy woman. She had a photoshoot for a fashion magazine in less than an hour and her hairdresser, Dante, was stuck in traffic on the M1. She stared at her reflection and swore. Her long jet-black hair hung in rats-tails around her face. Dante was never going to make it in time, and there was no way she was facing the press photographer looking like this.

She called to her PA, Julia Burton. "The hotel must have someone!" she shrieked. "It's supposed to be five-star."

"I have already asked twice. The salon is booked solid all day."

Lana slammed the hairbrush down on the dressing table and swore. "That's not good enough! Don't they know who I am? Don't they realise the damage I can do to this place? I tell my thousands of followers about this catastrophe and both the hotel and this stupid town will suffer. No one will want to come here ever again!"

Julia stood behind her employer and lifted a lock of limp hair. "Do you want me to have a go?"

Lana Midani's eyes widened and she shook her head. "No! Your hair is dreadful. There's no way I want to end up looking like you. Why did I come to this Ryebridge place anyway? It is nowhere, no one has heard of it. Why did you arrange this for me?"

"Because you thought it was a good idea, remember? You said you have a lot of fans up here in the North and this is a typical northern town, plus don't forget the TV appearance later."

Lana pouted. "It's local TV, a news programme, not mainstream. I'm not happy, Julia. This isn't right. These people are morons."

She stood up, regarded her reflection and frowned. "I'm going to have a word with the manager of that salon. He should know that his business will suffer if he crosses me."

"The people from the magazine will be here in a few minutes," Julia said.

"I don't give a damn about the stupid magazine. Tell them to wait. I want my hair fixing first."

* * *

He used the emergency staircase to avoid the CCTV. Just as well he was fit, it was eight floors up. But he wasn't prepared to take any chances. Shame he'd had to speak to the girl on reception. He'd have preferred to avoid that. But she was young, uninterested, had her face glued to a mobile the whole time. If she recalled anything at all about him, it wouldn't be much. He'd told her he was here about the dodgy lift. Without even a second glance she handed him a pass card and pointed him in the direction of the corridor. How stupid people were, and what a wonderful asset that was.

He kept his head down, his gloves on and his cap pulled down low over his face. Even if the police did spot him, they wouldn't be able to make much of what they saw.

Lana Midani had taken the penthouse. In a place like this it was expensive but not a fortune. This was Ryebridge after all, not Manchester. He was still amazed that there was so much money to be made from doing nothing, simply being popular. But that's exactly what she'd done. Springing from

25

nowhere, Lana Midani had charmed an entire generation. Thousands of teens across the globe were under her spell. Kids the world over copied her clothes, her make-up, even her exercise regime. In a way he admired her. After all, she'd fought her way to the top of her game, much like he had.

His plan was straightforward: enter her suite, finish the job and leave the way he'd come — simple and effective. He'd paid well for information on her movements today and wasn't anticipating any problems. He'd been told that Lana would be alone, working on her next social media campaign.

He rapped on the penthouse door and got his first disappointment. The woman who answered was not Lana Midani. This wasn't in the plan, and there was no time to consider an alternative.

The woman looked him up and down. "You must be from the magazine. You're early. Lana isn't ready and to be honest, she's not in the best of moods either."

Magazine? That was unexpected too, but given the circumstances, fortuitous. Why not? He had to cover his tracks and being a magazine reporter was as good a way as any.

He smiled at her. "That's a shame, because I have another appointment soon."

"Are you on your own? We were expecting at least a reporter and a photographer."

The man shrugged. "There's only me, I'm afraid."

"Look, you'd better come in. I'll ring, tell her you're here. I'm Julia Burton by the way, Lana's PA."

A PA. He'd been told she'd be out of the way. Wrong information, for which someone would pay. And there was this interview in the offing, another thing not passed on. But she'd invited him in, which was something. It would get him out of the corridor and away from any prying eyes. "Is Lana here for long?"

"Only for this shoot with you and a TV interview tomorrow. We'll be heading back to London after that," she replied. "Can I get you a coffee while you wait?"

He nodded. "Great, thanks."

He saw Julia get a good look at his face before she turned her attention to the coffee. She could give the police a reasonable description.

"Where's your equipment — your camera and the like? You could get set up while we wait for Lana to return." Before he had time to think of an excuse, Julia picked up her mobile. "She's gone to see the manager of the beauty salon. With you coming, and the shoot, she had a right strop about her hair. I'll see if I can reach her, tell her to hurry back."

The expression on Julia's face told him that Lana wasn't picking up. He had to draw a line under this and make his exit. Lana Midani wasn't here and if she was having her hair done, she could be hours. This woman asked too many questions, plus experience told him she was the observant type. He had no choice but to abort the job for now, but he couldn't just leave Julia behind. He'd have to clean up.

As Julia turned to pour the coffee, he stepped forward and grabbed her from behind. For a few seconds, she struggled to free herself from his grip but he was too strong for her. She didn't even have time to scream. The blade went in quick and deep, between the ribs and straight into her heart. Julia slid to the floor. Problem solved. It was a pity, she wasn't meant to die. Her only mistake — being in the wrong place at the wrong time.

CHAPTER SIX

Over the next few hours, the CID office was a whirl of frantic activity. Colin spent most of his time on the phone. He spoke to Dean's course tutor who sent him a list of the students in his group. He rang round them all, asking what they knew about Dean. One of them, a lad called Dave, told him that Dean had recently been to see a solicitor called Rob Connor. Dave had no idea why, said Dean was very secretive about it. Colin wrote Connor's name on the board and looked him up on the system. He checked with the Commodore Hotel, where the woman he spoke to sounded upset. She said they thought a lot of Dean and that he'd be missed. Colin told her he'd be round to interview the staff as soon as possible.

Harry was busy checking the names and faces that featured on Dean's bedroom wall. Dean seemed to have had a theory that their unknown killer was responsible for all the murders whose victims' faces he had posted on those boards. The Greenwood family had visited Galashiels. Was that where Dean had first become aware of the killer? The more Harry considered it, the more he thought it likely that Dean met his end because of what he knew. The killer had wanted to silence him. For ever.

"The girl from Hulme?" he asked Jess.

"Killed in her home, same method as the Scottish killings, a single thrust with a knife, straight into the heart," she
said.

"Is that all that links this lot? That they were all stabbed?"
Harry was puzzled.

"That, and they're all on Dean's board," Jess said. "We
don't have anything else yet."

"Are we saying the killings are random? Wrong place,
wrong time?" Harry grimaced. "Dean was a teenager, how
did he find all this out?"

"The neighbour told us Dean had noticed a man that
he'd seen in Scotland hanging around. Perhaps his suspicions
started then, and he began to wonder what the man was up
to. We have his board and the clippings, but we don't know
or have any proof that the murders are the work of one person," Jess said.

"We have to find out, and quick. Check the PMs and
forensic reports for those we know about."

"I've read through the gory details in the Galashiels
murders file." Jess shivered. "Two men, both stabbed in the
lodge they were renting. One managed to crawl outside and
bled to death out in the open."

"Did forensics or the PM throw anything up?" Harry
asked.

"Nope. The killer left no trace. The man who crawled
outside was in the open overnight and the wildlife had got
at him. They found no prints or DNA, other than that of
the victims. One was a middle-aged bloke and the other a
teenager. The older man was a known drug runner in the
town. They were together in the holiday park lodge when
the killer struck. Both were knifed, PM findings confirm it
was the same blade, and there were no witnesses. I've spent
a good couple of hours reading the files. The police up there
put it down to a fall-out among dealers. I can't find any
link between the victims, apart from the way they died and
where."

"Did the police find any drugs?" Harry asked.

"Only traces on some of the surfaces," she said.

"Dean and his family were in that park at the time," Harry said. "Dean might have seen or heard something. The killer considers him a danger and follows him to Ryebridge. He must have contacted Dean for them to meet up. What I don't get is why Dean put himself in danger like that. Everyone who knew him thought he was a bright lad."

Jess shook her head. "That's pure speculation. We have no proof that that's why the killer came here or that it's the same killer as in Scotland."

"Well, he must have had a reason. We have several murders, all fairly local to here. I doubt it's coincidence. Dean told his neighbour that he thought he was being followed," Harry said. "Perhaps he was, and the killer thought he knew more than he was comfortable with."

"So, the killer follows Dean and decides to knock off a few more while he's in the area? There are times when I wonder about you," Jess said. "What we should be looking for is a link between the victims, because there has to be one. You're all over the place with the job at times. We have to work with what we've got, not what we think could be the case."

"I trust my instinct," Harry said.

"You can't do this job by applying instinct alone, Harry. We investigate, find the evidence that'll hold up in court. You're the one having fanciful ideas now, which makes it all the easier to believe what Sandy Munroe said that day."

Sandy Munroe had told Jess about the death of Harry's twin brother in a house fire that killed their father, and how he'd dragged Paul out of the burning building. Sandy had a theory that his brother Paul switched places with his identical twin, and that it was Harry, the detective, who'd died. A theory that needed burying if Harry was to get any peace.

"Perhaps Sandy is right and I'm so inept because I'm still finding my feet." But his attempt at making light of it fell flat. Harry saw the look — she'd obviously given it some thought. "What Sandy said then has nothing to do with this case. You'd do well to forget it. Sandy would say anything to serve his own ends."

"I didn't say I believe there's anything in that little speech he made," Jess said.

"Good, because the only reason he said those things was to mess with your head. He wants to destroy my career, nothing else. And before your imagination goes into overdrive, my brother Paul Lennox was killed in that fire, not me, and Paul was no detective, take my word for it."

"What did he do for a living?" she asked.

Harry didn't want this conversation to go any further, but Jess wouldn't give up. He supposed she was bound to have questions after what Sandy had told her.

But she gave him a nudge. "Okay, you can drop it now. You've made your point."

He grinned. "Good, because I wouldn't want my reputation tarnished."

"What, that you made it to DI by sheer fluke?" Jess laughed. "Too late, Lennox, everyone knows that."

"Got me banged to rights, haven't you?" he said.

"You didn't answer the question. What did Paul do?"

She was back at it. "He was self-employed, a painter and decorator," Harry replied. "Bit flaky where hard work was concerned but he did okay for himself, kept the wolf from the door. Now let's move on."

Harry's eyes were back on the incident board. "Something links the victims, or he kills randomly. So which is it?"

"What about the others, the potential victims?" Jess asked. "Choosing them beforehand isn't random, it's premeditated. We can check the ones he's killed, but as for the other three, we've no idea how Dean knew about them."

"Complex lad, our Dean. For now we'll do what you say, investigate what we've got. It would help if we had a clearer picture of Dean, and what he knew, before we can work out what he was up to," Harry said.

"You're right, Harry. We can start by speaking to that solicitor in town, find out what Dean wanted with him."

Colin Vance joined them. "Seems Dean was an introvert," he said. "He didn't get on with his classmates but he was an exceptionally bright lad. He achieved top marks and was tipped to go far. His tutor reckoned it was his 'know it all' attitude that made the others dislike him."

"Any names in particular come up?" Harry asked.

"No, they all tended to keep away. In any case, Dean was always working on some project of his own."

"And we know exactly what that was," Jess said.

Harry was worried. If Dean had been right, there were three people on that wall who were still in danger — one unknown, Lana Midani and the man with no face. Harry wondered who would be next on the killer's list.

"Right, guys," he said to Jess and Colin. "Lana Midani will have to be told and offered protection. We need to speak to her urgently."

Jess smiled. "I'll come with you. I wouldn't mind meeting the famous Lana myself."

CHAPTER SEVEN

They were halfway down the stairs when they heard Colin call out, telling them to hang on. Harry stopped and turned round. Colin stood at the top of the stairs, looking flustered.

"There's been a murder at the Metropole," he shouted. "A woman's been found dead in her room."

Harry closed his eyes for a moment. This was what he'd wanted to avoid, but he'd delayed acting until they'd got more details. Now it looked like it was too late. "Do we know who?" But Harry knew already.

"No, but the victim was found in the penthouse."

"Lana," he groaned.

"The manager rang it in," Colin said. "He sounded shaky, kept going on about the amount of blood."

"The killer got to Lana first. We should have moved faster." Harry was furious with himself. "You drive, Jess, and I'll organise Melanie. We should have stopped this."

"Let's get there and find out what happened before we jump to conclusions," she said. "We're still working things out. That information on Dean's wall is all well and good but there's not much of it. Just faces and the odd note. We need more than that. For all we know, Dean simply collected the information on the victims and selected the others because they were people he didn't like."

"You don't really believe that. The lad was onto something." Harry still blamed himself. Had they acted when they'd first seen that wall, perhaps they could have prevented the murder. "Now we've got yet another body for forensics to pick over, and that's not what I wanted."

"A few days away hasn't sweetened your temper much," Jess said. "Glasgow not what you expected?"

"I didn't go to Glasgow," he said.

"I thought you went to see family."

"My family don't live in Glasgow, that's just where I used to work."

"Go on then, enlighten me," Jess said. "Where *do* you come from?"

"You wouldn't know it, so it's a waste of time me telling you."

Harry could understand her curiosity. After that last meeting with Sandy Munro and what he'd said, he was surprised Jess hadn't pumped him for information before now.

"I might. I have been to Scotland, you know."

He sighed. She wasn't going to give up. "It's a small place by the west coast, on the Cowal peninsula. Dunoon."

"You're right, I don't know it. You shouldn't be so wary of telling me stuff, you know, Harry," she said gently. "I'm your friend as well as your colleague. If there's a problem, something you're hiding . . ."

She meant this. Harry knew that Jess would help if she could, but she was better off not knowing anything. "It's not that simple. Where I'm concerned, ignorance is best. That way, you're not implicated. You have your own career to think about."

"Now you're speaking in riddles. Why not just come clean? I know you lost your father and twin brother to that fire, hence the burns and scarring on your hands." She paused. "But I know there's more. Sandy said as much." She took a breath. "I was there with you at that last meeting,

Harry. I heard what he said. He cast doubt on which twin walked out of that burning building — you or your brother. Harry or Paul."

This was a conversation he didn't ever want to have, and particularly not with someone he worked with. "I thought we'd just sorted that one."

"You can't kid me, Lennox. You're hiding something and it's eating you up."

"Now you're talking rubbish."

"I don't think so. Something else happened that day, and you refuse to talk about it." She cast a sideways glance in his direction.

Harry was looking out of the car window. "Too damn right it did," he muttered.

"If not the fire, is it to do with that character Mungo Salton? I remember him coming up in the last big case we worked on."

She remembered, did she? How could he forget? That villain haunted him, day and night. "Leave it, Jess."

This was getting out of hand. He wasn't comfortable with Jess prying into his background or the people he once knew.

"I got his name from an old colleague of yours in Glasgow, but he didn't say much, so I looked him up. Salton is a big-time villain with links to nationwide organised crime. He's some enemy to have. I'm not surprised you're scared."

"He's retired, and I'm not scared," Harry said, almost inaudibly.

"Villains like him never retire, you know that," Jess retorted. "And if you're not scared, why hide yourself away in a dump like Ryebridge?"

Jess was too close to the truth for comfort. He'd transferred to Ryebridge because it was a quiet anonymous backwater where, with luck, no one would find him. After what had happened to his family, he needed some breathing space. Then Sandy Munroe had exploded into his new life and almost wrecked it.

Sandy had been Harry's friend and mentor during his time at the Glasgow station. But an honourable retirement hadn't been enough for Sandy. He'd defected to the dark side and thrown in his lot with a people-trafficking ring, a case Harry and Jess had investigated. At their final meeting Sandy had said he wanted to explain, but instead he'd opened up a whole can of worms. What he'd said about Harry was dynamite and could have blown his new life apart. Harry was surprised that Jess had kept so quiet these last few weeks — she had to have questions. Well, she did. She'd obviously being doing her homework while he'd been away.

They drove the rest of the way in silence. By the time they arrived at the hotel, the top floor penthouse had been cordoned off. They were met by a uniformed officer who showed them into the plush accommodation. The body was lying just as the killer had left it.

"That's not Lana Midani," Jess said at once. "This woman is a lot older."

"She's Miss Midani's PA," a uniformed PC explained. "Ms Midani was in the beauty salon downstairs at the time. She found the body when she returned."

"Where is she now?" Jess asked.

"In a room down the corridor with some bloke who reckons he's her hairdresser."

At that moment Melanie and Hettie arrived from the Reid. "Seen all you need?" Hettie asked. "Only you're contaminating the crime scene."

"Let's go and speak to the girl herself," Harry suggested.

CHAPTER EIGHT

Lana Midani was sitting on a sofa weeping, her head on a young man's shoulder.

"We'd like to speak to you about what happened today," Harry said and showed her his warrant card.

"No pictures, I insist," she said, putting a hand in front of her face. "I look a state."

"We have no intention of photographing you, Ms Midani," Harry said. "We aren't fans, we're not press, we're police. All we want is to ask you about Julia Burton."

She stuck her nose in the air. "I have no idea what happened. I wasn't here. All I know is everything has gone horribly wrong." Ignoring Harry, she turned to the young man. "Dante, I can't do this, all these questions. I can't cope without Julia. She does it all, arranges everything. I'll be a complete mess without her."

"Julia Burton, your PA," Harry said sternly, "has been murdered and like it or not, you'll have to answer our questions. Did she say anything to you about being afraid of anyone? Maybe she noticed someone watching the pair of you."

Lana shrugged. "She said nothing, so I can't help you. Perhaps it was a robbery and Julia got in the way."

"We don't think so. Think carefully, Ms Midani. Has anything out of the ordinary happened during the last few days? Any strange phone calls, or have you thought you were being followed? This is important."

"No, nothing. Like I said, I can't help you. I wasn't here!" She was shrieking now. "Don't you understand? I went down to the salon to give that imbecile who runs it a roasting, and when I returned, Julia was dead."

She buried her head in Dante's shoulder and began to sob. "It was dreadful. Julia was just lying there on the floor, with all that blood everywhere."

"Did you see anyone? Did you pass anyone when you got in or out of the lift?" Harry said.

"No. I didn't see anyone. I have no idea why this has happened or who could have done it."

Harry was growing tired of her attitude. Did she think she was above answering a few simple questions? A shake-up might help. "We have reason to suspect that the intended target was you, Ms Midani."

That had its effect. She gasped and jumped to her feet. "What for? Why would anyone want to kill me? The whole world loves me."

"Not quite," Jess said. "Can you think of anyone you may have upset recently?"

"Not enough to want me dead. Sometimes if things aren't right, I shout. I have standards." She pouted, then it seemed to dawn on her. "I don't understand why this happened to Julia, but if it was me the killer was after, he might try again. I want protection. You must keep me safe!"

"And we will." Jess smiled at her. "But the accommodation may not be quite up to your usual standard."

Lana frowned. "I can't stay just anywhere. Not me." She paused. "I'll make my own arrangements."

"No, we will make them for you," Harry said. "And it'll have to be quick. You can't stay in your suite. The forensic people will have to do their work."

"I'll tell the manager to put me in another one then."

"We will put you in a safe house. You'll have one of our family liaison officers with you. It'll be their job to update you should there be developments," Harry said.

"That sounds like I'm being put in prison. I won't have it. I don't care what you say, I want to go home. I'll be safe there."

"If we're right and you are the intended target, the killer won't give up. He'll follow you to London and try again," Jess said. "He killed Julia, next time it will be you."

Lana pulled a face and sighed. "If it's absolutely necessary then I suppose I'll have to do as you wish. But I'm not happy, now get out of my face."

Ignoring her rudeness, Jess turned to the young man. "Who are you?"

"Dante. I am Lana's stylist. I just arrived, so I missed the incident. I literally walked in to find police all over the place." He disengaged himself from Lana and kissed her cheek. "It might be better if I wait downstairs."

After he'd shut the door behind him, Harry turned to Lana. "You said you found Julia. How long were you gone?"

"I was having my hair done," Lana wailed. "I came back to the suite and there she was, lying in all that blood. I spoke to her, felt her pulse, but there was nothing." She shuddered. "Who could do that, and why kill her?"

"I think she was killed because she saw him. She must have answered the door, and they'll have spoken. If he'd allowed her to live, she'd have given us a description," Harry explained. "How long did the hair thing take? An hour?"

Lana Midani flashed him a withering look. "I don't know. I didn't sit there watching the clock."

"I simply want to get my head round the timeline. The killer must have believed you'd be in your suite."

"And I would have been if Dante had arrived on time. But he was late, so I went downstairs to see if the salon here could do my hair. I had to look my best — I was about to be interviewed by a magazine."

"What magazine?" he asked.

"I have no idea, Julia saw to all that, but it's a local one, published in Manchester."

"Had Dante arrived on time, what would have been the routine? Would Julia and him have stayed with you?"

"I only asked Dante to come last night. If things had gone to plan, he'd have finished long before the interview and have been on his way back. It was Julia's day off — she was going to go shopping in Manchester. She only stayed with me because I was in a flap about my hair," Lana said.

"Why didn't you simply stay at the Commodore in Manchester? It belongs to the same chain," Jess asked.

"They were full, so they offered us a suite here at a reduced price. Julia said it was a good deal and close enough to the city."

Finding Julia here would have thrown the killer. If he'd found out about Lana's plans and those of Julia, he'd have expected her to be alone. Harry wondered how he knew that much.

"Do you know what happened to the reporter?"

"I have no idea. He never arrived. Julia will have left word with reception to expect him and allow him to go up."

So that was how he got to her. Whoever had arrived earlier and gone up to her suite was no reporter. "It would be useful to know more about the arrangements for the interview," Harry said. "How and when they were made. Did Julia have a laptop she used? I'd like to check her emails."

There was one lying on the coffee table. Lana picked it up. "Take it, but please let me have it back. It'll have my diary for the next few weeks on it."

Harry and Jess stood up to go. "I'll leave a uniformed PC with you. We'll arrange new accommodation and ensure your safety."

"I'm still not happy about being incarcerated in some crummy flat somewhere," she said.

"It's for your own good. You should understand that the killer will know full well that he's made a mistake. If he decides to put that right and try again, you must be somewhere we can protect you. You must cooperate, Ms Midani. Your life depends on it. I'll speak to you again shortly. Meanwhile, discuss it with your friend Dante. We'll get one of the uniformed officers to send him up. Perhaps he can make you see what's in your best interests."

"Quite the little diva, isn't she?" Jess whispered once they were out of earshot.

"Spoilt brat more like," Harry said. "We'll get protection sorted for her. Dean was right about her being a prospective victim, though it's a mystery how he knew."

They returned to Lana's suite to find Melanie bent over the body of Julia Burton. "He's good, I'll say that for him. One stab straight to the heart, exactly like the Greenwood lad. She didn't have time to put up a fight, the attack must have been a surprise. There are marks on the front of her neck. It looks like he surprised her from behind, put a hand around her neck, pulled her round and stabbed her between the ribs."

"The good doctor's take on events is sound," Hettie said. "The problem is the lack of forensics. There are no prints on the door or any of the surfaces, only Ms Midani's and those of our victim. I think she offered him a drink — see? The cup is set out ready. He must have struck when she turned her back on him."

"What? No prints at all, not even the odd stray hair?" Jess asked.

"We'll be doing a fingertip search of this place, so we'll see what turns up. If I get anything, you'll be the first to know," Hettie said.

"This guy is ultra-careful, isn't he?" Jess said to Harry. "He does his best not to leave forensic traces and he doesn't risk leaving witnesses who can describe him either. Hence Julia, the PA, had to die."

Jess had to be right about the PA, but Harry was sceptical about the forensic traces. "They always leave something behind, Jessie," he whispered. "What the forensic team have to do is find it, no matter how small it is."

"I'll let you speak to Hettie about that," she said.

The forensic scientist was across the room, examining a blood spatter on the wall. "Would you compare the wound with Dean's?" Harry asked. "I'd like an opinion on whether the same blade was used."

"I'll let you know about her PM," Melanie chipped in. "We're planning to do Dean's in the morning."

Harry handed Hettie the laptop. "This is Julia's. Will you pass it to IT forensics, ask them to see what emails went back and forth between Julia and an alleged reporter?"

Hettie nodded and bagged it.

"How did the killer get up here?" Jess asked. "D'you reckon he took the lift?" She went out into the corridor. "Look, there's a camera up there in that corner." She turned to the uniform who was stopping people coming onto the floor. "Would you check with the manager about CCTV? We want a copy of any footage from this afternoon."

CHAPTER NINE

There were three people on duty at the reception counter. Harry wanted to speak to whichever of them had checked in a man asking to see Lana.

A middle-aged woman in a dark suit introduced herself as the reception manager. "She's had no visitors today, other than her hairdresser. If she had, we'd have told you at once."

"Ms Midani was expecting a reporter," Harry said.

"We're aware of that, but he or she never checked in with us."

"Are people allowed to wander in and out of the hotel at will?" Jess asked.

"Of course not. Guests leave their keys when they go out and pick them up from us on their return. Everyone else has to check in here. They are asked their business, their names are put on the system and they are given a visitors' pass." Shoulders back, she raised herself to her full height and glared at Harry. "We're very security conscious here, Inspector. We can't have all and sundry just wandering around the hotel."

"But the killer did just that. He came in, went up to the penthouse and killed Ms Midani's PA."

Her eyes narrowed. "Sharon! Come here, girl."

43

A teenage girl joined them. She was wearing the same uniform but her skirt was much shorter.

The woman immediately laid into her. "A man — a stranger, not a guest — came in here today. He may have asked for Ms Midani. Did you let him go up to the penthouse?"

"No, she had no visitors."

"You're sure, Sharon?" Jess asked. "You might have been busy. He could have got past without you noticing."

"Not possible," the manageress said. "To get through that door over there and into the rest of the hotel you need a key card."

"Did you issue a key to anyone who wasn't a resident?" Harry asked.

"Only the bloke who came to mend the lift," Sharon said.

Now they were getting somewhere. "Did he give a name?"

"No. He said he was the engineer so I gave him a key."

"How many times do I have to tell you!" the manager shrieked. "You always get their details."

"Can you describe him?" Jess asked, ignoring the woman. "Think hard, Sharon, this is really important."

She shrugged. "I didn't really see him. I was, er, dealing with a call at the time."

The manageress's face was red with rage. "More like you were playing that damn game you're so fond of on your phone. Get your coat. You know the rules. I'll deal with you tomorrow. How many times do I have to tell you young people? Leave your bloody mobiles at home."

"He was wearing motorbike leathers with boots to match," Sharon piped up. "I do remember that because they suited him. Dead fit he looked."

Fit or not, this man was a killer, and they had to get him before anyone else died. Harry and Jess went to have a look around, trying to work out which route he would have taken up to the top floor.

"I doubt he'd use the lift — more chance of being picked up by the cameras. There's the main staircase and the emergency one. Place like this, there'll be CCTV on the main one, let's hope the other's covered too," Harry said.

They headed towards the lift. "How d'you reckon Dean knew? D'you think the killer could be a friend of the Greenwoods, or a relative?" Jess asked.

"We need more information. Until we get something solid, it's all just guesswork, Jessie."

"Should we still look for possible links between the victims?" she asked.

Harry shook his head. "By all means give it a go, but I don't think we'll find any. There's the geography for starters, and they are all very different people — their ages, their jobs, their sex, everything."

"So why does he choose them, Harry? Are they simply random kills? Lana Midani is high profile — take her on and it'll attract publicity. He must know that."

"Perhaps that's what he wants, Jess — the whole world to know what he's capable of and how clever he is. He's certainly got some nerve, I'll give him that."

They set off up the emergency staircase, all eight floors of it.

"There are cameras," Jess noted. "One on each floor. With luck, we should get a reasonable image."

"I think he's far too clever for that," Harry said. "It's possible he checked this place out prior to today — to know the whereabouts of this staircase, he'd have to. It's tucked away down a corridor and not signposted from reception."

"It should be," Jess said. "What if there's a fire?"

CHAPTER TEN

Jess sounded increasingly frustrated. "Regardless of who else this maniac has killed, we've got two bodies and nothing to work with. How does he do it? I hope Hettie finds us something."

Harry understood Jess's disappointment but was more optimistic. This man's luck was bound to run out. "So far, he's been extra careful, but remember, he's human. He will slip up."

"But can we wait until he does? We have Dean's 'incident board' with four dead faces local to us and two in Scotland. I've checked each and every one, and the cases are still open. He hasn't slipped up yet."

"Col is looking at them, checking again to see if there are any links between the victims. He might find something we can use," Harry said.

"Our best bet is Dean himself," Jess said. "He knew things about the killer, that's why he died. Being the lad he was, Dean must have kept records. What we have to do is find them. My money is on those laptops."

"If there is anything to find, IT forensics are up to the job," Harry said.

"That solicitor, Connor. Want to speak to him before we go back?" Jess asked.

Harry nodded. A word with him and then back to the station to see what they'd gleaned since this morning.

* * *

Rob Connor had an office on Ryebridge Road. The place was empty, apart from a young woman of about eighteen with short blonde spiky hair wearing a Ryebridge Academy blazer. She looked up from one of the computers when they entered.

"If you want my dad, he's out," she told them, stifling a yawn. "I've no idea when he'll be back but he'd better be quick, I'm knackered."

"We're police," Harry explained, hoping that might make her more helpful. "We're here about Dean Greenwood's murder. We believe he spent time with your dad."

The girl shook her head, smiling. "No, he didn't. Dean came here to see me. I'm Thea Connor."

"You and Dean were friends?" Jess asked. "His mother didn't mention you."

"That's because she only saw us together a couple of times," Thea said. "We hung out sometimes, that's all. Dean wouldn't have told his mum much, he didn't want her sniffing around. He didn't like anyone getting too interested in what he was doing."

"And what *was* he doing, Thea? Chasing a killer is a popular theory," Harry said.

The girl shrugged. "Dean could be a bit weird. He told me about that, but I didn't take much notice. I just thought it was Dean being his usual paranoid self."

"And now? Since his murder?" Harry asked.

"Seems a bit iffy, doesn't it?" The girl was grinning. She didn't seem at all upset that her friend was dead. "Looks like he really pissed off someone this time."

"If he didn't want his mum to know, when did you meet up?" Jess asked.

"We didn't, not that often anyway, but usually in the library in town, or if his mum was working, at his."

"And what did the pair of you get up to?" Harry asked, raising an eyebrow.

"Nothing much. He could be okay, a bit of a laugh, but then he'd get all intense. Like I said, Dean thought he was chasing a killer. Sometimes we'd meet in the library, have a coffee in the café."

"Didn't you see any merit in his research?" Harry asked.

"You've seen his room, his wall. You must have realised he got all that stuff from the papers. It doesn't prove much, but Dean made this big conspiracy out of it, decided he was on the trail of some serial killer. He had someone in mind too, although he never told me who it was. The mistake Dean made was telling *him* — well, the man he thought was him. I reckon the guy was some lowlife who felt threatened by Dean's ramblings, and that's what got him murdered."

"Thea, d'you know anything at all about this man? Any details that might help us? His name, for example?" Jess asked.

"No. Dean never said. He might not have known himself." She looked at them and frowned. "Can't be easy for you lot."

"No, it isn't," Harry said. "So you think Dean's wall means nothing at all?"

"His faces? Yeah, just cut-outs. He reckoned there were more, he just didn't know who. Dean told me that he hadn't pieced it all together but he had a good idea who the killer was. I did warn him. I told him that if by some stretch, he was right, one day this bloke would do him real harm." She shrugged again. "I was right too."

"Do you know if Dean kept any records, notes of what he'd discovered about the victims and the killer?" Harry asked.

"Yeah, course he did, Dean was meticulous, noted everything no matter how small. That's what the three laptops are for. One he used only for gaming, said it kept him sane during the small hours. Night owl, you see. Another was strictly for research and the third for his notes."

"Couldn't he do all that on one?" Jess asked.

"Course, but that was Dean. Neat, tidy, everything in its own place, even this project."

"You said three laptops," Harry said. "We only found two in his room."

"Well he had three. I should know, I watched him use them often enough."

"You've seen his notes?"

"Only some," Thea said. "Gibberish mostly, at least to me. He wrote in code. Careful to a fault was Dean."

"Did Dean tell you anything about his plans for the night he was killed?" Harry asked.

Thea Connor shook her head. "He didn't want me tagging along so he never said much. Like I said, I did warn him. I told him that if by any chance he was right, then this man was dangerous. But Dean wasn't having any. He said that him and this bloke had an understanding and that he'd be quite safe."

"That suggests Dean had arranged to meet this man, spoken to him. Do you know how he set that up?" Jess asked.

"Who knows? Dean had been stalking him for a while. His plan was to blackmail the bloke, get money out of him for his silence. That's when we fell out. Dean was taking things too far. I wanted him to stop, didn't see the sense in it."

"Surely Dean must have realised the danger he was putting himself in that night?" Harry said.

"Well, Dean's dead, so I can't ask him. He reckoned he had something that'd ensure his safety, something to trade. I dunno. Dean believed it gave him the edge and he wanted to use it to get money out of this man."

"Any idea what that edge was?"

"No. The entire plan was a bad idea and I told him so. Whoever this man was, I doubt he was a killer like Dean thought. Doesn't make sense, does it? If he was, you lot would be chasing him. But whoever he was, he'd had enough and must have decided to put an end to Dean's interference once and for all."

"So Dean never used the killer's real name," Jess said.

"Not with me. Perhaps he didn't know it."

"On Dean's wall there's a blank face. D'you know who that is?" Harry asked.

"No idea. *The faceless man* is what Dean said the killer called him."

"How did Dean know that?" Harry asked.

Another shrug. "Can't help with that one either. Dean made stuff up and he could do the secretive thing well."

Harry saw the smirk on Jess's face. She was thinking the same about him. "D'you know if Dean ever met the killer, spoke to him about the deaths?"

"He never said anything to me, but he could have done."

Harry stuck a hand in his jacket pocket and pulled out a card. "If you recall anything else, Ms Connor, give me a ring. We need all the help we can get on this one."

"I'll ask his mum if she knows anything about the missing laptop, but what's the betting she doesn't," Harry said as they made their way back to the car.

"So, where is it? D'you think it's been stolen?"

"Highly probable, Jess. Dean could have had it with him that night, or someone took it from the house. I'll get Hettie to do another sweep of that bedroom."

"Back to the station?" Jess asked.

"Let's hope Col's got something, because from where I'm stood, things are just getting worse," he said.

"Don't fret. Melanie is doing Dean's PM tomorrow. That might give us something," Jess said.

But Harry wasn't holding his breath. This case was turning out to be a right bugger, which was borne out by Colin Vance back at the station. The young DC had spent all afternoon checking the background of every victim but had found nothing to link them.

"They are all very different," he told Harry and Jess. "Different backgrounds, different jobs . . . this guy here lives in an exclusive apartment block near Wilmslow, but her," he pointed to another, "she's from a social housing estate in Hulme."

Col was right. There was nothing at all that connected them. It made no sense, and it was giving Harry a headache.

"Sir," the duty sergeant called from the office door. "You have a visitor downstairs."

"We'll call it a day," Harry decided. "Jess and I will attend the PM in the morning. Col, you chase up IT forensics — we're desperate for the information on those laptops we found in Dean's bedroom. And then we'll carry on the good work here."

Harry went down to reception to see who wanted him. The sergeant pointed to a side room. Hopefully, this would be quick. All Harry wanted was a meal and some peace and quiet to think. But when he saw the woman waiting for him by the window, he knew that wasn't going to happen.

CHAPTER ELEVEN

"Isla! What are you doing here?"

Seeing her standing there gave Harry a massive shock. His heart was thumping so hard he thought she must surely hear it. She looked no different — the same jet-black hair and slim figure. Alone at night in the quiet hours, this was the woman he thought about — Isla, and what might have been.

Now, she looked him up and down as if trying to work out what had happened for things between them to end this way. There was no disguising the hurt she still felt. Her accusing blue eyes stared into his very soul, seeking the explanation he couldn't give her. In another life she had known him better than anyone. Did she see the truth now?

"You didn't visit," she said, her tone sharp. "You were home but never came near. D'you know how much that hurt me?"

"Sorry, I didn't have long. A couple of days, that's all. Work, you know how it is," he mumbled. It was a weak excuse and not the reason at all. Seeing Isla would have been the icing on the cake, but it wasn't without its dangers. He couldn't put her at risk.

"No, I don't know how it is," she said. "Why don't you tell me, help me understand what's going on? After everything we went through, the last thing I expected was for you to just . . . just walk away like that. You left me without a word. Nothing, not a call, not even a text. I had no idea how you were or where you'd gone, or even if you were still alive. Do you have any idea how that felt?"

Harry couldn't discuss it. The issue was too raw, cut too deep. "Isla, what are you doing here? I'm working, and I don't have much free time."

"Working? What at? I don't understand any of this. You should be at home, among people you know, people who love you." She gave him a small, tremulous smile. "I miss you."

"You miss Paul," Harry said. "It's not the same. He was my twin but we aren't the same person."

"You look like Paul to me."

"Well, I'm not, you've got the wrong twin, Isla."

She stroked his arm. "See the scar on your wrist, you got that scrambling over the rocks on Dunoon beach six summers ago."

Harry laughed. "Not good enough. I've had numerous scuffles, it goes with the job. I've also been caught in a house fire since then. I'm covered in scars." He wiggled his fingers at her. "Take a good look at these if you don't believe me."

"I've heard the rumours," she said angrily. "And I know the truth. I've worked it out and I need to talk to you. I won't be fobbed off."

He had to cut this short. The duty sergeant was listening in, practically with his tongue hanging out. "Not now, and not tonight. I'm too busy. Where are you staying?"

"I'd hoped to be staying with you," she said. "I haven't arranged anything else."

"I'll get you a B&B. How long are you here for?"

Her eyes glistened with tears. He hadn't handled this well, had he? Harry shook his head.

"I'm up to my eyes in a tough case, otherwise—"

"You don't fool me. I know you too well. We were engaged, we still are." She flashed her ring at him. "Or had you forgotten!"

Without another word, Isla Stewart spun on her heel and left the room. Harry stood, looking around. The desk sergeant had been hanging on every word. There was no stopping it. The juicy bit of gossip about Harry's young woman would go round the station like wildfire. How would he explain this one in the morning? And what tale could he spin for Jess?

* * *

Until recently, Harry had been living in a campervan on a mate's drive. During the last case he'd worked on, it had been deliberately set alight, rendering him homeless. Since then, Harry had been staying with Colin Vance. The young DC was so grateful to have made the team at last that he'd been only too pleased to offer Harry his spare room.

Colin's home was a brand-new apartment, and he had the habits to go with it. Col was tidy. He cooked all his own meals and shopped for a week's worth of food at a time. He washed his shirts after one wear and ironed them as if he was branding them. Colin always looked the business. Not Harry's style at all. That Colin was fast coming to resent his boss's sloppy habits became more obvious as each day passed. But tonight, Colin was out. He was meeting up with some old college friends at a local pub. It gave Harry an opportunity to relax, order some fast food, down a couple of cans and chill in front of the telly. What Col didn't see wouldn't hurt him.

The plan was a shower, trackies on and order that pizza while downing the first can. Harry needed to numb his mind from the hassle of the day. First there was the case, and now there was Isla. No way could Harry have her poking around in his new life. But how to stop her?

Harry got out of the lift on the third floor to be faced with Hugh Devereaux, their neighbour. He was a tall, dark-haired fit-looking man. Harry put him in his mid-thirties, like him. Hugh was struggling with a pile of box files.

He smiled at Harry. "Bringing work home is a right pain. And it's got to be sorted before tomorrow."

Harry nodded. "Your job sounds as bad as mine. But in my case, tonight is for chilling. Too much thinking doesn't do any good."

"Difficult case?" Hugh asked.

"And then some. We've got a serial killer and a list of potential victims."

"Nasty. I don't know how you deal with folk like that. All that death. It must leave scars."

Ignoring the remark, Harry said, "I'm sending out for pizza. Fancy one?"

"Nah. I've got something in the fridge, thanks. I'll eat and read. I have to be word perfect for tomorrow. I'm one of the speakers at a seminar in Manchester. Outlining new dental procedures to the latest bunch of recruits to the profession."

Harry grimaced. "Sounds like a load of laughs."

Hugh grinned. "Each to his own, but I do enjoy the job, even the travelling about. I'm off again next week, be gone a few days."

"CID isn't much better," Harry said with a wry smile. "Let one of us know when you're back and we'll get the beers in."

"Good night, Harry," Hugh said, turning the key in his lock. "I'll drop you a text."

Harry watched him disappear into the flat. He'd have to temper the noise now. No having the telly on loud if Hugh was trying to concentrate. But he didn't mind. Like Hettie had said, this was a far cry from the camper and Harry was grateful to Col for taking him in.

CHAPTER TWELVE

Day Two

The following morning, Harry met Jess in the car park at
the Reid. The moment he caught her eye, he saw the amused
look. She knew. Already.

"Someone's told you."

"Oh yes, you're the talk of the station, Lennox. Black
hair, very pretty. Scottish, I heard. I'm guessing she's someone from back home. And — the big news — you were
actually engaged. Want to tell me about her?"

"No, so don't even try."

"Apparently you weren't very nice to her. Seems she left
the station with a flea in her ear. That's no way to treat an
old girlfriend."

"She's not an old girlfriend, and she was engaged to my
brother, not me. Which is a pity because I did have a thing
for her too, but it's too late to turn back the clock now."

"The duty sergeant said—"

"Will you leave it, Jess," he snapped. "I'm not up to this
right now. I'd rather think about the job in hand if it's all
the same to you."

"Okay, if that's what you want. But she'll be back, you know she will."

Yes, he did, Isla wouldn't give in. She wanted answers, so when she put him on the spot his story would have to be good. But his mind wasn't up to working it out. Not now. Isla would have to go on the back burner until he was ready.

Melanie and her team had Dean Greenwood laid out ready on the table. "He's been officially identified by his mother," she confirmed.

The lad was tall and slight. In death, his skin was pale with a waxy sheen. The burns had left red, raw patches on his midriff.

"When the petrol caught, the initial flare burned through the clothing covering his chest."

"Did the knife wound kill him?" Harry asked.

"Let's find out." Melanie measured the width and depth of the wound.

They watched her make the usual incisions in the body and remove the heart. Turning the organ around in her hand, she said, "I was right. The wound is catastrophic. The killer used a thin blade, double edged. It went in between the ribs and straight into the heart. Death would have been quick. He didn't suffer and would have known nothing about the fire."

"Anything else?" Harry asked. "Bruising, defence wounds for example?"

Melanie turned over each of the hands. "There's nothing. I doubt he saw this coming."

Harry sighed. "Is there anything you can give us that'll help? So far, we've got two victims and a killer, with nothing to link any of them."

"We'll swab for DNA, but I doubt we'll find anything. The fire, plus the rain . . ." She grimaced. "But we'll do a full tox screen, see what that throws up, if anything."

So far there was nothing helpful. Their killer knew what he was doing and not to leave traces behind, but Harry couldn't believe there was absolutely nothing. Dean was a bright lad. If he'd been at all suspicious of his killer, he'd have reacted. He'd been on this man's tail for a while, he must have known how dangerous he was. "Check the Greenwood house again, see if you can find that missing laptop, and go over his clothing a second time, will you?" he asked.

"On it," said Hettie. "What's left of it. There's mud and blood, as you'd expect, but so far, it's only the lad's."

"Anything on the boat?" Harry asked.

"It's been badly damaged by the fire," Hettie said. "But on the upper side, near the edge, we did find a partial boot print. It matches those we found on the lake bank and along the muddy trail that leads back to the playground." Hettie pulled a face. "We've taken casts, but boot prints alone aren't going to help much. We need the boots themselves to put the owner at the kill site — provided he hasn't cleaned them or dumped them somewhere."

Melanie was still examining the body under the bright lights.

"The blade used to kill him — have you checked it against the wound inflicted on Julia Burton?" Jess asked.

"Yes. Although I haven't done the full PM yet, I have looked at the wound. I'd say the same blade was used for both killings," Melanie confirmed. "Same thickness and depth of wound."

So, that was it. Dean's PM yielded nothing apart from the fact that the same blade probably killed him and Julia Burton. "Let me know if anything else turns up," Harry said as they left.

The pair made their way back to their cars. "The CCTV from both the playground and the hotel should be in by now. I'll check it over when I'm back," Harry said.

"Even if you do spot him, I bet it won't help," Jess said. "He's clever, careful, he'll simply be a dark shape in the shadows."

CHAPTER THIRTEEN

Colin Vance knew that looking for links between the victims was a thankless task without something to work with. But where Lana was concerned, he believed he had just that. He'd been studying the case notes on the killing in Hulme and noticed a strong physical resemblance between Lana and the victim, Nadia Nasir.

Researching Lana should be simple — the young woman had a huge social media presence and her own YouTube channel. There were pictures galore, but that's as far as it went. There wasn't any real information, such as her family members or even where she came from, which was what he wanted. Nadia Nasir had lived and worked in Hulme on the outskirts of the city for five years, but the notes said she originally hailed from London.

Placing photos of both girls side by side, Colin was struck by their similarity. Unlike Lana, Nadia wasn't wearing a lot of make-up, but both had the same lustrous black hair and huge dark eyes. But it was more than that. There was something about the shape of the face and the high cheek-bones. It wasn't just that they shared the same ethic back-ground, Colin felt sure the two were related in some way. But if so, how?

He did a search of the birth, marriage and death registers, found the entry for Nadia's death, but no birth or marriage records, and there was nothing at all for Lana. It was possible that they'd been born elsewhere, or Nadia had changed her name. Regarding Lana, he had no idea. They'd have to ask her. But first, he had to make sure he was on the right track. He rang Hettie.

"There was a murder a month ago in Hulme — a young woman, Nadia Nasir. Would you do a DNA comparison with Lana Midani? It's just a hunch but I think the two women are related."

"No problem. Nasir's DNA will be on the system and I took a sample from Ms Midani myself for elimination purposes after the incident at the hotel. Put up quite a fight she did too. Seemed to think I was up to no good and it would jeopardise her freedom in some way."

"She could be right. I can't find any birth records for her or Ms Nasir," Colin said.

"You should speak to immigration. It's possible they are both illegals."

If that was the case, is that what got Nadia killed, and was it the reason for the attempt on Lana's life? And did that mean they had an ongoing dispute with a people smuggler? But what had that to do with their killer?

The DNA would take a while. Colin considered his next move. Harry liked initiative and Colin wanted to impress the boss. Dare he go and see Lana himself, ask her outright about Nadia? Colin decided to leave that one for now. He watched some footage of her on YouTube. Lana Midani was beautiful, opinionated, and she terrified him. Colin decided he'd look at the CCTV from Cheetham Park instead. The camera on the lakeside booth yielded nothing. It hadn't worked in months, apparently. Colin turned to what they had from the entrance.

On the night Dean was killed it had been raining, so the footage was dark and indistinct. The time stamp put Dean in the park at seven thirty, and a coloured flash on the side of his trainers made him easy to identify. He walked in front of the camera, hands in his cagoule pockets, hood up, and then disappeared out of shot. Five minutes later, a man strode within camera range, but the footage was so indistinct Colin couldn't get a clear sight of him. A few seconds later he saw him join Dean under the trees. The man was tall and wore bulky dark clothing, possibly motorbike leathers, with a hat or hood pulled well down over his face. Dean didn't show any surprise when the man appeared. He even smiled at him. They evidently knew each other.

Colin zoomed in on the figure and got a grainy partial side shot of the face. Suddenly, the interchange between the two men altered. The unknown man seemed to be trying to pull Dean back towards the entrance gates. But the lad was having none of it. Dean lashed out, shrugged him off and stalked towards the play equipment. The rain was now pelting down, and the quality of the video worsened. Colin squinted and stared but he couldn't pick up either of them again.

But he had that image of the face, such as it was. Colin printed it out and stuck it on the incident board. His next task would be to compare it with whatever they had from the hotel.

Lana Midani's suite was on the eighth floor. The footage came from the cameras on the emergency staircase, there was one on each of the eight floors up to the penthouse. At first, the stairs were empty and then a man came into shot. He was wearing motorbike leathers with heavy boots and a baseball cap pulled down over his face. He was tall and lean, but that was all Colin was able to gather. Was this the person who'd met Dean in the park? Colin couldn't tell.

Harry and Jess barged in, interrupting the peace and quiet of the office. "We got nothing from the PM," Harry told Colin. "Hettie's still got tests to do — toxicology and the like. What've you been up to?"

"I think Lana was related to the girl that was killed in Hulme," Colin said. "See these photos?" He laid them out, side by side. "There's a definite resemblance. I've done the usual checks, but I can't find any trace of either of them."

"I think you could have something there. Well done, Col. Want to follow it up? Go and question Lana, then speak to whoever is investigating the Hulme killing."

Colin nodded. If he could only get over being starstruck, he'd like nothing better than to meet the famous Lana. "There's that, too." He pointed to the other photo on the incident board. "Whoever he or she is, they were in the park with Dean the night he was killed."

"They look older than Dean, and much taller, but that's all I can make out. I don't recognise them."

Harry walked closer to the board and studied the image. "I do," he said soberly. "That's Brian Isherwood, the bloke who lives next door to the Greenwoods."

"In that case, Isherwood has some explaining to do. Why didn't he tell us he saw Dean that night?" Jess asked.

"More to the point, what was he doing there?"

CHAPTER FOURTEEN

"What's the man playing at? Why didn't he tell us when he had the chance?" Harry stared angrily at the image on the board for a few moments. "We'll bring him in, interview him formally."

"There might be a logical explanation for why he was there," Jess said.

"Then why the secrecy? No, he comes in. In the meantime, Col, look closer at Isherwood. His personal life, his job, everything."

"I'll make a start now," Colin said.

Harry needed to think. Not only was Isherwood in the park the night Dean was killed, he had also been in Galashiels when the Scottish murders occurred. Was he the killer, and had Dean been able to assemble his board because he was close to the man? If so, Isherwood would know what Dean had on him. Was it Isherwood who'd taken that third laptop?

Harry watched the footage from the park again. Did Isherwood know there was a camera? He made no attempt to hide his face. At one point, despite the rain, he pushed the hood back off his head. "We'll get round there," Harry said to Jess. "But I want another word with Dean's mother first."

"Why? What's on your mind?"

"That is definitely Isherwood. He didn't tell us he was there that night and that's suspicious in itself. If he is the killer, he knows Dean collected chapter and verse on him, and he wouldn't want that information falling into our hands."

"What about Lana Midani?" Col asked.

"We'll get round to her, don't worry. You'll still get a chance to meet the lovely lady."

It was a short drive to Isherwood's house, but it gave Jess enough time to ask about his visitor. "Your girlfriend gone back home then?"

"I've no idea, but I hope so. I don't have time to social-ise, not even with Isla. And she's not and never was my girl-friend," he lied.

"A drink wouldn't do any harm. She's come a long way to see you, surely you owe her that much."

"I owe her nothing. You don't know what you're talking about, Jess. Isla is history, and not mine either."

"I don't understand you at times, Harry. The woman was upset. The least you could do was talk to her properly. Whatever it is you're hiding, this isn't the way to deal with it."

"Don't tell me how to sort my life, Jess. I know what I'm doing."

"No, you don't, you're fumbling around in the dark without a clue. You're a mess, Harry Lennox."

* * *

Maggie Greenwood was at home. They saw her car on the drive and her face at the window.

"What're you hoping Maggie can tell us?" Jess asked as they approached the front door.

"What she knows about Dean's laptops, Isherwood — anything that might help," Harry said.

"Do you have any news for me?" Maggie asked as she opened the door. "Have you found who did that to my boy?"

"Can we come in?" Harry asked.

"Please, tell me why you're here," she insisted. "I don't think you realise how hard this is for me. Dean was my only child, my perfect boy. I miss him terribly."

"We're still investigating," Jess told her. "I know you're desperate for results, but believe me, so are we."

They moved into the sitting room. Maggie was weeping again.

"How well d'you know Brian Isherwood?" Jess asked suddenly.

Maggie looked from one to the other of them. "He's been a good friend to me and my Dean. Why?"

"Has he been living next door for long?" Jess asked.

"A couple of years or so. Him and June have been a godsend. They're the ideal neighbours."

"What does he do for a living?" Jess asked.

"He works for a horticulture company, selling seeds to garden centres and nurseries. He travels a lot, sometimes he's gone for the entire week."

"Away a lot then, and all over the country?" Jess said.

"Yes, but that's not unusual." Maggie frowned.

"Did he ever ask to borrow one of Dean's laptops?" Harry asked her. "We understand from a friend of his that he had three, but we only saw two. We suspect that there's important information on the third one."

Maggie Greenwood looked at Harry and shook her head. "What is this? What are you trying to do, blame Brian for what happened? Well you're wrong! Brian is a good man, he would never hurt my Dean!" She was shouting now.

CHAPTER FIFTEEN

As Harry and Jess left the Greenwood house, they saw Brian Isherwood on his drive, about to get into his car.

"Mr Isherwood, we'd like a word," Harry called out.

"What is it now?" Brian smiled.

"We want you to come down to the station, look at some CCTV we've got and answer a few questions," Harry said.

"Can't I do that here?"

"I'm afraid not," Harry said. "Everything checks out, we won't keep you long."

Isherwood's face clouded. "And if it's not, what happens then?"

Jess opened one of the rear doors and beckoned him over. "Sit in here next to me. The sooner we get this done, the better."

"This is way over the top. I don't know what you think I've done, but you're wrong."

"Let's hope so," Harry said.

* * *

Back at the station, once he'd been finger printed and a DNA sample taken they put Brian Isherwood in an interview room, while Harry went to get the stills from the CCTV footage.

"A call came in from IT forensics while you were out," Colin told him. "A woman called Sasha Steele wants to speak to you."

"I'll ring her when we're done here. About those laptops, is it?"

"Yes. I don't recognise the name. Is she new?"

"Don't know, Col. If she is and you want the lowdown, then you should speak to Hettie." He smiled. "Steele? If you do speak to Hettie, ask if this Sasha is related to Hector. He's the main man at the Reid. If she is, we'll have to watch our step."

Armed with the photos and a whole lot of questions, Harry went to speak to Brian Isherwood. He was seated under the watchful eye of a uniformed PC but didn't appear bothered. If anything, he seemed more curious than nervous.

"Should I have a solicitor?" he asked when Harry sat down. "Only I don't know any, and it might take me a while to arrange one."

"We can get you the duty one if you wish. It'll take about half an hour," Harry said.

Brian Isherwood thought for moment and then shook his head. "No, let's just get on with it. I've got things to do, as I'm sure you have."

"You're here, Brian, because we've examined the CCTV from the night Dean was killed." He gave the man a few moments to consider this and explain, but he offered nothing. "Minutes before Dean met his death you met him on the park and the pair of you spoke. That conversation got heated. At one point you were both arguing, you grabbed him, tried to pull him away." Harry watched him closely. Isherwood didn't seem particularly bothered by this revelation — not the reaction Harry'd been expecting.

Eventually, Brian Isherwood gave a sigh. "Okay. I haven't been altogether honest with you, Inspector. I knew what Dean was up to and I wanted to stop him. He confided in me a month back, said he was on the trail of a killer." He smiled at Harry. "But that was Dean. I'd seen his wall. Whatever he thought he was doing, I doubted very much that the man he was after was really a murderer. Even so, what he was planning was far too dangerous. He'd identified someone and had been following him. I have no idea who this man is, but if he took exception to Dean's fairy-tales, it could well get him into more trouble than he could handle. Dean was clever but his mind worked in strange ways. He got fixated on things, was guileless, he believed all he had to do was face the man with the so-called evidence he'd gathered and this stranger would hand over a small fortune."

"Why didn't you contact the police, tell us what you knew?"

Brian Isherwood spread out his hands. "Dean tried that. Check the records if you don't believe me. He had a conversation with one of you lot a couple of weeks back. He told the officer he was chasing a killer and they needed to act fast to save lives."

"What happened?" Harry asked.

"Nothing," Brian said. "Well, the lad had no name, no proof that would stand up. He had a lot of press cuttings and notes but nothing that wasn't already out there in the public domain. I reckon your colleague thought Dean had a screw loose."

Fair comment. "You spoke to Dean that night, then what?" Harry asked.

"I left him to it. Wrong I know, and I've regretted it every waking minute since. We argued and I lost it. I told him how stupid he was and stormed off. To be truthful, I thought it might do the lad some good if this man he was following gave him a pasting and knocked some sense into him."

"But it wasn't a fantasy, was it? Dean was right, he had discovered a killer and planned to meet him that night. I've been told that Dean had set up the meeting to blackmail the killer, which you just confirmed. He, however, had other ideas and now Dean's dead."

"If I'd known what was going to happen, I'd have stayed with him, tried to help."

"Did you see anyone else in the park when you were there?" Harry asked.

"Not a soul. The weather was foul, and I couldn't wait to get home."

"Weren't you concerned when Dean didn't come back?" Harry asked.

"I had no idea he hadn't returned. Maggie didn't come banging on the door until gone four in the morning. She'd been waiting for Dean but had fallen asleep on the sofa downstairs. When she woke up, she presumed he'd come home and gone straight to his room."

"If you thought Dean could be in danger, you should have contacted us at once, and told us what you're telling me now. At the very least, you should have come clean when he was found dead."

"But I didn't. I thought it was all in his head. I'm not proud of keeping quiet, but I didn't think anything I had to say would help. Besides, I didn't want Maggie to know I was there. If she found out, she wouldn't trust me or June anymore, and right now she needs us both."

Brian Isherwood's explanation sounded plausible, but Harry was still uneasy about him. There'd been no hesitation, he'd recited his tale as if he'd rehearsed it. At least Harry could check the records and see if Dean really had been in and reported his findings.

"You were also in Galashiels when the two murders happened there," Harry said. "Bit of a coincidence that."

Now Brian Isherwood looked angry. "Yes, it is, but I'm no killer, Inspector. This is getting silly now. Me being in Scotland at that time is because I was on holiday with Dean and his mum."

"Nevertheless, I want a list of your whereabouts over the last six months. All the places you stayed in and the people you met."

"You're asking me to provide alibis for the other killings?" Isherwood sounded shocked. "You can't really believe those murders were down to me!"

"You travel for a living, go all over the country. You knew Dean. You have access to his home and his laptops — one is missing by the way. I'm afraid you are very much in the frame, Mr Isherwood. You will be staying with us for a little while longer. You'll sit here with my colleague and do that list, after which we'll speak again."

CHAPTER SIXTEEN

Harry left Isherwood and returned to the main office, where Colin and Jess were studying the images of Lana and Nadia Nasir.

"Explain himself, did he?" Jess asked.

"Yes, but I'm not convinced. He's doing us a list of the places he's been and where he's stayed during the last few months. We'll have to check the lot," Harry said. "You two got anything?"

"You can't really think Lana Midani is here illegally?" Jess asked Colin. "Unlikely, given how well known she is."

"But if she is, and Nadia is too, then that could be why there's a bounty on their heads," Harry said.

"Lana is a wealthy woman. Perhaps she was being black-mailed and didn't pay, so Nadia was killed and she was next," Colin suggested.

"We have no proof of that," Harry said. "But whatever the reason, we need Lana to talk to us."

"But if Lana is afraid of something, or someone, she'll refuse, won't she?" Jess said.

"Want me to try, boss?" Colin asked.

"Okay. You and Jess go and see her while I talk to Sasha Steele. Be careful, don't let her play you. Lana Midani craves publicity and you're about to hand her a shed load on a plate." Harry picked up the office phone. "Now, let's hope Ms Steele's got something useful from Dean's laptops . . . DI Harry Lennox. You wanted a word?"

"I'm working late at the Reid," Sasha said. "Can you come over?"

"Fine, give me half an hour." Harry turned to Jess. "I'll pay her a visit. You and Col see what Lana has to say, and then you can call it a day."

* * *

"I'll ring, tell her we're coming," Colin said.

"No, let's just turn up," Jess said. "If the lovely Lana is hiding something, we don't want her disappearing or taking to her bed before we get there. We'll take the photos of Nadia. They might shock her into talking to us."

"You think she knows who's behind this?" Colin asked.

"I think Lana knows more than she's told us, Col. People have a nasty habit of hiding stuff when they deal with the police."

"Want me to drive?" he asked.

"It's only the other side of town," Jess said. "Get your jacket. It's not a bad day, we'll walk."

"We will get him, won't we?" Colin asked as they left the building. "He's been active for a while and so far, no one's come close."

Jess wanted to reassure him that it was only a matter of time, but she really wasn't sure. This one was no ordinary murderer. He planned before he struck, researched each victim. His were no spur of the moment, in-a-fit-of-anger killings and, despite what Harry might say, that made him unlikely to slip up.

She shrugged. "We can only do our best."

* * *

For her own safety, Lana had been moved into a safe house outside Ryebridge, but she wasn't happy about it. Not having a suite in a hotel with people to wait on her hand and foot didn't suit her.

As the family liaison officer let them in, Jess and Colin could hear Lana shouting the odds.

"What's upset her now?" Jess whispered to the FLO.

"The food isn't to her liking, and I'm afraid I'm no cook."

Lana strode towards them down the hallway. "This place hasn't been cleaned properly," she said. "There was a spider in the bathroom this morning. I can't stay here any longer. You have to complete your enquiries. I must go home."

Colin was surprised at how quickly she appeared to have got over the murder of Julia Burton. Spider in the bathroom indeed. What about her safety? All that filled the young woman's head was her own comfort.

"I deserve the best," Lana complained. "I've worked for it. This house . . . Her." She nodded at the FLO. "She doesn't understand me. If any of this gets out, the bad publicity will do serious damage to my image."

"Your PA was murdered," Jess said. "You seem to have forgotten that you, not Julia, were the intended target."

Lana looked sceptical. "You don't know that."

"Oh, I think I do, and I have good reason for it," Jess said. Colin thought of Dean Greenwood's bedroom wall. "So, it's time to be candid with us. Who've you upset, Ms Midani? Why would someone want you dead?"

Lana gave Jess a filthy look and tossed her head. "No one! I am loved the world over. Haven't you seen my social media profiles? I'm telling you, you've got this horribly wrong."

"Where were you born?" Colin asked.

"London." She looked surprised at this sudden question.

"Have you ever changed your surname?"

She scowled at him. "No. Why would I?"

"Then you weren't born in London, or even in this country. I know because I've checked. You have no past, Lana. Why is that?"

She glared at him. "You're talking rubbish. Of course I have a past. I come from a perfectly normal family. You need to look at your records again."

"Do you know a young woman called Nadia Nasir?" Colin asked.

Lana turned pale. "How do you know that name?"

"More to the point, how do you? And don't lie to me. I can see from your face that you're hiding something."

"Where is Nadia?" she whispered. In complete contrast to the Lana of a few minutes ago, her tone now was almost pleading. "Contact her for me, tell her where I am, and get her to ring me. I need to speak to her."

"Sorry, Lana, I can't do that." Colin saw the look of disappointment on her face. "I'm afraid Nadia was murdered a month ago."

The killing had been reported in the local press but living in the South, Lana wouldn't have seen it. For a few moments Lana was silent as she took in the significance of Colin's words. Then she closed her eyes and began to wail.

"She can't be. It's not possible. I would have known. How come I didn't feel it?" She gave Colin a long, sad look. "Nadia was my sister."

He'd spotted the resemblance in the photos, but he hadn't expected Lana to admit it so readily.

"I've been looking for her, we'd lost touch lately," Lana said. "I am everywhere on social media. She must have seen me, so when she didn't try to make contact, I thought perhaps she was ill, and I got worried."

"Why did you lose touch?" Jess asked.

"We just did. Sometimes life is like that. I was working hard and I didn't have time to think about what she might be doing." She paused. "How did she die?"

"The same way as Julia Burton, and we think she was killed by the same man," Jess said. "First your sister and now your PA. So you see, you have to take this seriously, Lana. Your life is in danger. You must trust us to do what's best for you."

"Do you know why this man killed them?"

"No, but like we said before, Julia wasn't meant to die. After Nadia was killed you were the next target," Jess said.

"Perhaps Nadia wasn't meant to die either. He made one mistake — he can make others," Lana said.

"We have certain evidence to prove he intended to kill Nadia. He wanted to kill both of you, both sisters. Why, Lana? There's something you're not telling us, isn't there? What is it?" Jess asked.

Lana Midani stuck her nose in the air. "Nothing! There's no reason why anyone would want me or Nadia dead."

"You're lying, Lana," Jess said. "We can't help you if you're not straight with us. Tell us about your past, where you were born and how you got to this country."

"I cannot do that."

"Are you here illegally, Lana?" Colin asked.

"You think that's why Nadia is dead and why I'm on some *hit list*? Because we're illegals? God, you're a pair of fools!" she shouted.

The scorn on her face seemed to be genuine. Okay, so she wasn't here illegally. "Tell us then, help us to understand," Colin said. "Two years ago you appeared out of nowhere. You became successful, and now you're a wealthy woman. Is someone blackmailing you, Lana? Did they demand money, you didn't pay and that's why your sister is dead?"

"That's a load of nonsense," she said, sounding less certain.

"I don't think so. You can talk to us. You're quite safe here, no one will find you." Jess waited. "Okay, we'll give you a little more time. But you will tell us the truth, Lana, about you and Nadia, where you came from, the lot."

The young woman looked beaten. The news of her sister's death had hit home and all her fight had evaporated. Lana sighed.

"I don't have a choice, do I? I don't want to die like the others. I will cooperate, but I haven't done anything wrong." She seemed to brighten a little. "And while I'm here, I want to stay in touch with my followers."

"Out of the question," Jess said. "You must not phone anyone, send a text or go online. That's all it would take for the killer to find you. Do you understand?"

Lana gave a reluctant nod.

"We'll talk again, and if you need to know anything, speak to the officer who's living with you."

On their way out, Colin had a word with the FLO. "I'm going to put a watch on the house. It's vital that no one apart from us gets in or out. Do you understand? That young woman is in danger and while she's here, she's our responsibility."

CHAPTER SEVENTEEN

Harry was right. Sasha Steele was related to Hector. She was his daughter.

"It's okay," she assured him. "I don't tell tales. I'm temporary, here on loan, so make the most of my knowledge and my time."

Harry chuckled. "You're good then."

Flashing him a smile, she came back immediately. "The best you're going to get in this little backwater."

"Fair enough. Better lay it on the line then. The laptops belonging to Dean Greenwood, the murder victim from the park. We're hoping they'll tell us how he found out so much about a killer we're after."

"Well, he didn't find him online," she said, disappointing Harry. "And believe me, I've looked damned hard. There are any number of dubious sites on the dark web where you can find such people, but Dean didn't go near. As far as I can make out, he never used the Tor browser or interacted with anyone through a dodgy forum or chat room. This laptop," she tapped it, "is full of arcade games, but the one on my desk is what Dean used for his research. He was a clever lad, careful about deleting his history, but I've managed to recover most of it. When I first saw the websites he'd visited,

I admit I was confused. His favourite was a site for selling second-hand goods. He spent hours there but, as far as I can see, he never bought or sold anything,"

That wasn't what Harry had expected to hear. The dark web, yes, but second-hand goods on the normal web? It made no sense. "Well, I'm stumped. I was convinced the killer was touting his wares on the dark web and that's where Dean found him."

"There are any number of sites at the dodgy end of cyberspace that the lad might visit to find such people, but like I say, there's no history of him going there."

"We know there's a third laptop which is missing. According to a friend of his, that one has his notes on it."

"Then I suggest you make finding it a priority," she said. "The answer to why he visited the buying-and-selling site could well be in his research notes."

Harry was looking at an example Sasha had brought up on screen for him. "I don't understand. This is an advert for toys. How was that supposed to help Dean find out who the killer's next victim is?"

"Not just toys, Harry, miniature cars, the type serious collectors look for. Who knows, perhaps the lad wanted to start a collection. Anyway, he stumbled across your killer somehow, but not on the dark web." Sasha sounded dismissive. "I'll email you the web addresses of everything he spent time looking at over the last couple of months, but there's a lot of it, I warn you."

"Thanks, Sasha, though I don't know how it'll help us. Dean got his information from somewhere and I doubt the killer told him. So what was he up to? How does a teenage lad find an experienced killer if he doesn't find him in cyberspace?"

"Well, failing the dark web, perhaps they used some sort of code. I'll look again at that selling site, see if I can spot something. Who knows?"

"I'll check over what you've found, see if it makes any sense." Harry smiled at her. "You worked hard, found some possibly useful stuff. I'm grateful." He liked that Sasha was friendly and that she didn't look at all like her father. She was easy on the eye and he'd noticed that there was no ring on her finger. Her one irritating habit was the fact that she couldn't keep still. She stood at her desk rather than sit, and was constantly pacing the lab, drinking coffee while she talked.

"Your lad was clever," she said, "but he gave himself away, or the killer laid a trap for him. Shame. If things had been different, Dean would have gone far."

"He was studying IT at college," Harry said.

"There you are then."

Sasha made for the kettle and flicked the switch. "My next job is finding out if Dean knew how the killer was paid. I'm presuming it would be in bitcoin. I'll let you know if I get anything on that score from his laptop."

"This entire thing is still a puzzle," Harry said. "Even if the killer was contacted through some sort of coded message in an advert, there are still the details to be got."

Sasha took a mug from a shelf. "Want one? We can thrash out the possibilities."

Harry shook his head. "Got to get back," he said, and grinned. "Haven't you drunk enough of that?"

"It's what keeps me going. I've got another twelve hours in this place to do yet."

"Twelve! You must like your work," Harry said.

"Oh, I do, and I want to see what else I can get from these." She tapped the laptop again. Harry noticed that her nails were plain, short and unvarnished. Unusual these days.

"I've interviewed a neighbour of Dean's," he said. "He had opportunity, motive too, if Dean was proving bothersome, plus they were close. He could be our man."

"Worth another chat?" she suggested.

"Thanks, Sasha. You've given me a lot to think about."

She smiled at him. "Find that third laptop and I'll be even more helpful."

CHAPTER EIGHTEEN

Day Three

The following morning Colin, who always left the flat before Harry, told him Lana Midani had been on the phone, asking for whoever was in charge. "She's not happy, boss. Reckons hanging around in a run-down house at the back end of nowhere — her words not mine — is doing her head in."

"But she only spoke to the both of you yesterday. Couldn't she have told you then?"

Jess grinned. "Oh, we're mere minions. Lana wants to divulge the big stuff to the boss."

"Big stuff?"

"Despite the Nadia issue," Jess said, "and being told her sister was murdered, she still doesn't seem to understand the danger she's in. A bit of plain speaking is what's needed."

"Okay, point taken. Col and I will speak to her about Nadia and how they got into the country. While we're gone, would you contact the Galashiels police and see if they can add anything to what we already know about the killings up there?"

"You mean the big fat nothing, like all the other murders this guy is responsible for."

"We'll get there," Harry assured her. "It's only a matter of time." But he'd said this more to ease his own anxiety than anything else. This case was difficult. They were up against a cool-headed killer who wasn't making mistakes.

"Rodders has visitors," Jess said. "I only caught a glimpse as they swept through the office, but they've been in there talking ever since."

"Did you catch what they wanted?" Harry asked.

"No, but I got the impression Rodders knew one of them. Ray, who's on the desk downstairs this morning, said he's from the Greater Manchester Serious Crime Squad."

What did they want? It wasn't unusual for the super to have visitors, even ones from a high-profile station like that, but Harry wondered why they were here now. It made him a little worried. The last thing he wanted was that lot sticking their noses into his case.

"Grab your stuff, Col, we'll get off."

"Want me to find out what they want?" Jess asked. "No guarantees, mind you. Rodders doesn't usually confide in the likes of me."

"You mean a lowly DS," Harry teased. "Don't beat yourself up, he doesn't tell me much either."

* * *

"I should be back in London. I've got commitments," Lana complained. "You say I'm not safe, but why would this man want to kill me? I haven't done anything to him."

"You're not safe, and we still have questions for you that need answers."

She folded her arms. "I can't tell you anything."

"I think you can, Lana," Harry said. "You can start with the reason why Nadia was murdered."

"I have no idea."

But her tone belied the look on her face. Harry was surer than ever that Lana was hiding something. "She wasn't just murdered," he told her, "someone tracked her down, researched her life, what she did, and then he struck when she was alone. Imagine how she must have felt — a young woman, terrified and with no one to help her."

Lana burst into tears. "Stop it! Stop torturing me. D'you imagine I don't think about Nadia? It should never have happened. She should have been with me. I begged her to come to London. I would have given her a job, looked after her, she'd have been happy."

"Why didn't she?" Col asked.

"Nadia wanted to, but she couldn't get away. She had to work. She owed some man a lot of money. I don't know why, I asked but she wouldn't tell me. She was terrified that if he found out about something she'd done, he'd kill her."

"Does this man have a name?" asked Harry.

"She never told me, said the less I knew the better."

"Are you sure the name didn't slip out in one of your conversations?" Harry said.

Lana shook her head.

"But she told him about you, Lana, didn't she? She must have, or why is the killer now on your tail?"

"That's just guesswork," she said.

"It's more than that. He kills Nadia, contacts you and demands that you pay what she owed him. He knows who you are and that you can well afford it. You refuse, so now you're top of the hit list," Harry said.

"You should talk to us, Lana, tell us everything you know," Colin added.

She looked down. There had been doubt in her big dark eyes. Harry had seen it. "He sent me a note," she admitted at last. "It didn't come in the post but was hand delivered. I came home one night and there it was, slipped under the door."

"D'you still have it?" Colin asked.

"No, I burned it."

"Can you recall what it said?"

"He wanted money. The note said I must pay what Nadia owed or he would kill her."

"And you really have no idea who this man is?" Harry asked.

"No. I said. Nadia wouldn't tell me."

"When was this?"

"Several weeks ago."

"And although you knew how frightened she was, you did nothing? You left your sister to suffer on her own?" Harry was amazed. "Didn't you at least tell someone, advise Nadia to go to the police? Or even go to them yourself?"

"I told Nadia to do that but she wouldn't listen. I had no details, no names, and I didn't even know where Nadia was working. The last time we spoke, Nadia said she was going to run away, hide at a friend's place until I could go and get her. I've heard nothing since."

"D'you know who this friend is?" Harry asked.

"No."

"You have different surnames. Why?" asked Harry.

"I wanted something different, something glamorous that went with the work I do."

"Why can't we find birth records for either of you?" Harry asked.

"We were born in Syria. Our birth parents were refugees, they came to the UK when we were babies. They both died young, and after a succession of foster parents, Nadia and I were adopted by the Nasirs."

"Your parents weren't illegals?" Colin asked.

"No. Look again and you'll find the paperwork. Our family name is Hakimi."

Harry handed Lana a notepad and pen. "Write down the last address Nadia lived at in Hulme."

Lana nodded. "If you find anything, you'll let me know, won't you?"

"That depends on what it is. Meanwhile, you must stay here and not risk trying to leave. Your life is in danger, Lana, you must do as we say."

They left and went back to the car.

"Think we've got it all, boss?" Col asked.

"Who knows with that one? But we've other stuff to think about. This man she spoke about, we need to find him, have him questioned. He may be our killer."

CHAPTER NINETEEN

Colin drove them back to the station while Harry sat and studied his notebook. The case was building. They had plenty to work with, but would it lead anywhere? Had Lana been honest? His instincts told him she had — up to a point, but she'd left out some important details. He'd go over everything she'd told them back at the office.

Before he went upstairs to his office, Harry took a detour to the canteen. He'd eaten very little all day and wanted something to tide him over. He was going to the local curry house with Col and Hugh later and intended to do the menu proud.

He'd just got a ham sandwich and coffee when Jess joined him. "I'd get up there if I was you. Rodders has been in and out of the office asking where you are, and that visitor of his is still with him."

He groaned and checked his mobile. He'd had it on silent while they spoke to Lana, so he'd missed the super's calls. He grabbed the food and followed her up. He put the sandwich in his desk drawer and swilled down the coffee, burning his tongue. "Col will fill you in about what we got from Lana. A couple of things need checking out."

He ran his fingers through his blond hair and straightened his tie. He'd no idea who Rodders's visitor was, but he had to be important.

He knocked on the door and waited until he heard the super call out to him.

"This is Superintendent Joe Weeks from Manchester Serious Crime Squad," Rodders said.

Harry nodded and shook the proffered hand, wondering what a super from that lot could possibly want at Ryebridge nick.

"Your team have been busy," Weeks said, clearing his throat. "Not done bad either. Turned up more than we have, and my lot have been at it for weeks."

He had to mean their multiple murder case. "Thank you, sir."

"I'd like you to come to HQ in town first thing tomorrow. Bring whoever it is you work with, and we'll go over a few things," Weeks said.

"That'd be DS Jess Wilde, sir."

"Well, make sure she knows and don't be late. We've a lot to get through."

Having delivered his instruction, Weeks collected his coat and briefcase and left.

"Hope he isn't going to pinch our case, sir," Harry said when he'd gone.

"We'll have to see. Weeks told me as much as he told you, so I've no idea what's on his mind," Rodders said. "But two of the murders are on our patch, and we're not giving them up easily."

Harry returned to the main office where he told Jess about Weeks, and their visit the following day.

"Is he going to stick his nose in?" she asked. "Take what we've got and tell us to butt out?"

Harry wouldn't be surprised if he did, but he didn't want the team giving up. "I've no idea. We'll have to wait and see. Want to pick me up about eight in the morning?"

"Okay, but if this Superintendent Weeks bloke tries to steal our case, I won't be happy. He must have given you some clue."

"From the little he said it sounds like his team are working the same case and have come up with very little. They probably just need a hand." He chuckled.

"They don't have Dean Greenwood's wall, do they?" she said.

True, but how long before they demanded he hand it over? And even if he did, would they find the missing pieces to complete the puzzle?

* * *

Thea Connor reckoned her neat little know-nothing act had convinced the two detectives that she was clueless about the extent of Dean's research. If only they knew . . . but they didn't, and that gave her an advantage. Dean had planned to extort money from the killer. Dean was dead. Now it was her job.

Thea was a clever girl. She'd worked it out. She had Dean's third laptop, the one the police were hunting high and low for. Not that it was easy to work out, because it wasn't — he'd written most of his notes in code. But Thea had managed to glean certain details, enough to know that a man called Ian Roebuck was next on the killer's list. The hit was to be later that night.

As well as Dean's laptop, Thea also had three spy cameras he'd owned. Those little beauties were just what she needed for the next part of her plan. What she wanted was video, positive proof of the killer going about his business. Then she'd do what Dean had planned, use the video to make him pay up. He'd have no choice, otherwise she'd go to the police. She'd be smarter and more careful than Dean.

Roebuck was a delivery driver for a local laundry company. He lived alone in a ground floor flat on the Baxendale. Thea had kept watch on his flat and asked a couple of the estate kids about Roebuck's routine. They told her that he went to the pub most nights and usually returned home in the small hours, drunk. He was a large man, vicious and bad-tempered, so his neighbours steered well clear. Confident that no one would dare enter his flat when he wasn't there, Roebuck had become sloppy. Thea had often seen him go out without even bothering to lock his front door. And when he did, he simply shoved the key under the mat.

She smiled to herself. There was no reason why this shouldn't go like clockwork. Her plan was to set the cameras up, wait until the killer had done his worst, then retrieve them and examine the footage. The killer wouldn't know what hit him. When he got the text and the attached snippet of video, he'd pay up all right. He'd have no choice. The money would be in her possession within twenty-four hours. Thea had worked with Dean, helped him with his research and reckoned she deserved the pay-off.

Back in the beginning, when Dean had told her about the killer and his plan to blackmail him, Thea had scoffed. She thought he was fantasising and questioned everything, but when she examined the evidence Dean had collected, she'd changed her mind. Dean was right. He had found a killer.

The plan to put cameras inside Roebuck's flat had been Dean's idea. What if the killer struck outside, she asked, while Roebuck was either on his way to the pub or coming back home? Dean had said that wouldn't happen. The killer had always struck indoors, where there were no witnesses and no CCTV. Ironic that Dean was the exception. She supposed it was his reward for pissing the killer off.

The three spy cameras looked like air fresheners. Roebuck was always so drunk he was unlikely to notice them. They would do the trick. They worked independently of Wi-Fi, were battery operated and used an SD card to store data. The only drawback — it meant a second visit to collect them once the killer was done. Thea wasn't looking forward to that part. It would be tricky, sneaking in and out before the police got wind of what had happened. Her timing would have to be spot on. And of course, there was the question of where to place the cameras. Thea reckoned one in the bedroom, another in the kitchen, and one that captured most of the living room.

CHAPTER TWENTY

Harry was tired, but he wasn't done for the day yet. Like it or not, he'd have to make sure he knew the case inside and out for when Weeks fired questions at him in the morning. He returned to Col's flat with a pile of paperwork. He'd do the homework first and then chill with a couple of cans. Col was out again, meeting his sister who had some major panic on her hands, and would be late back.

Harry got out of the lift. Isla Stewart was there, waiting for him. His stomach lurched. This wasn't in the plan, and she had that familiar look on her face, the one that told him she'd stand for no nonsense. Isla wanted answers he couldn't give, and he had no idea what to tell her. Not the truth, for certain. He began to panic.

"I thought we'd have a chat," she said firmly. "And I'm not going to be fobbed off."

She wouldn't either. Isla was a skilled interrogator. She'd been a DS on the force in Glasgow and had sometimes worked with Harry. He showed her the files. "You can see how I'm fixed. Look at this lot. I've got to read through it all before tomorrow morning."

She didn't look impressed. "Why won't you talk to me? I know you. You're hiding something and all this talk of work is simply delaying tactics."

"You're wrong, Isla. The case we're working currently is full on and I have to report to a senior officer in the morning. I don't know my stuff and it won't go down well."

"You're not fooling me. You're even using the same stupid excuses. You were never one for hard work — the easy option, that's your way."

"No, you've got it wrong. This *is* me. I've got a job to do, a killer to catch and that comes first." But the sceptical look on her face remained where it was. He had to get rid of her, tonight he must work, and even Isla couldn't be allowed to get in the way.

"I know the truth, about what you did, why you ran, why you're trying to change your life." She looked into his eyes. "You're running from Mungo Salton. This false trail you've laid, this story about you really being Harry won't stop him. I know that's rubbish and so will he."

"What if it isn't rubbish, Isla? What if it's the truth?"

"In your dreams."

She spun on her heel and stalked off towards the lift. He was sorry to see her go like this, but there was no alternative. Isla Stewart was yet another sacrifice to his new life.

* * *

The killer had done his research. He knew that Ian Roebuck could handle himself. He'd learned that Roebuck had been a boxer in the army and was no pushover. So he'd worked out how to minimise the risks. A small departure from the normal routine, but it was necessary. The killer was running out of time. He had been given a deadline and he didn't want to let the man who'd hired him down. The plan was to drug Roebuck and kill him while he slept. Sounded simple, but it still had its risks. There was no room for error. He'd get just one chance to incapacitate the man.

Roebuck was a drunk with a taste for whisky. After spending most of the night in the pub, he regularly drank several glasses of his favourite tipple when he got home.

Tonight, those drinks would be his downfall. The killer had laced the whisky with a tranquiliser.

It was gone midnight when Roebuck returned and found the gift-wrapped bottle on his doorstep. Without looking round he scooped it up and took it inside.

Parked in the shadows, the killer was watching the flat. He was counting on Roebuck not being able to resist, and that within a couple of hours he'd be lying comatose on the sofa.

The killer waited. He had to give Roebuck ample opportunity to drink from that bottle. Because of the crime and the perpetual trouble with teenagers, this wasn't a popular area even in daylight, and at night it was worse. The killer hunkered down and listened to engines scream as hyped-up adolescents raced each other around the dark streets in any car they could get their hands on. Most were stolen, he guessed, or illegal, and in any case, what was the betting not one of these joyriding kids was actually old enough to drive?

He listened with a wry smile, recalling his own adolescence. He'd been the model son. Private school had taught him manners which, combined with his good looks, made him popular, particularly with the girls. In another life he might have married the perfect woman and settled down to raise the perfect family. But domesticity, comfort, wasn't for him. No thanks. He played the part, maintained a relationship and held down a job of sorts for the sake of appearances, but that's all it was — appearances. He'd learned early on that women weren't worth the hassle of long term commitment. He enjoyed his work too much. A wife would ask questions, make demands, and he couldn't have that. He valued his solitude. And killing for a living was a much more exciting option.

She blended well with the surroundings, so he didn't notice her watching him. Dressed in dark clothing, she sat chatting with a couple of others in a gap between a row of garages. Just a group of bored kids waiting for their next fix.

How wrong he was.

Time to move. The killer got out of his car and went to Roebuck's door. As usual, Roebuck had gone in and left it unlocked. The hallway was in darkness — so far so good, but he could see light spilling from what he assumed to be the sitting room. The television was blaring away but there was no sign of Roebuck. A half-empty bottle of whisky stood open on the coffee table. It wasn't the one he'd delivered.

"Who the 'ell are you?" The gruff voice coming from behind him made him freeze for a second. "What you doin' in my 'ouse?"

Regaining his composure, he thought quickly. He smiled. "I'm a neighbour. A woman in the flat above thought she heard a scream. We were worried you'd hurt yourself."

But this cut no ice with Roebuck.

"It's the bloody telly — stupid mare." Roebuck squinted at the man. "Get out! Go on, and don't you dare come in 'ere again."

"Sorry. We just thought you might need help, that's all." The killer turned and took a step towards the door. He'd come back later when Roebuck had gone to bed. This man was tall and heavily built, and his mood was sour after a night's drinking.

Roebuck moved towards the killer and grabbed him by the scruff of the neck. "Rubbish. You're in 'ere chancing your luck. Now get out before I do you some serious harm."

The killer smiled. "I wouldn't if I was you."

Angered, Roebuck snarled, an animal about to pounce. He pulled the killer round and punched him hard in the face, knocking the cap from his head. Roebuck then threw him across the room. The killer groaned. He'd fallen backwards and didn't have time to find his feet before Roebuck hauled him upright and propelled him forcibly towards the living room door. Someone in the flat upstairs shouted and banged on the floor. He had to finish this now.

"Stop! You're making a mistake," he yelled.

Roebuck spun the killer round and pulled his right arm up behind his back. It felt as if it might break. "No mistake. Not me, mate. No one gets in 'ere without my say so."

He didn't have long. This would be messy, but it had to be done now. With his free hand, the killer reached for the blade tucked away in an inside pocket of his leather jacket. Roebuck was behind him, so he struck out blindly, missing the heart and stabbing him in the stomach. Roebuck released his hold and fell. But he wasn't dead.

The killer stood over him, smiling.

"Bad move that. Taking me on was a big mistake." Roebuck was bleeding heavily but he was still alive. "Goodbye, friend. Sorry to cause you pain. I'd hoped to make it easy, but never mind. It's over now."

He thrust the knife in between the ribs, going in deep and twisting the blade. Roebuck was dead. Snatching his cap from the floor, the killer left, closing the door behind him.

* * *

Thea Connor was a pretty hard cookie but going back into Roebuck's flat was one of the worst things she'd ever had to do. She'd never seen a dead body before, not even tidied up for a funeral, and the sight of Roebuck lying in a pool of dark, sticky blood made her want to be sick. His face was grey, his eyes wide open, staring, as if in surprise.

She'd waited until about an hour ago, when she'd seen a dark shape leaving the flat. This had to be the killer. Time to make her move, quickly, while there was no one about — no neighbours, and best of all, no police. With luck, it would be tomorrow before the killing was reported.

Thea went round the rooms collecting the three cameras, which she put in her bag. There was every chance she'd have something. The one she'd placed in the living room was pointed straight towards where Roebuck lay.

Job done, she took one last look at the body. She could have stopped this, gone to the police, told them what she knew. But where was the fun or the profit in that? "Sorry you had to die," she whispered, stepping over Roebuck on her way out.

Aware that the killer might still be around, Thea tagged along with a group of youths walking her way. Safety in numbers. It took her twenty minutes to reach her house. There was only her and her dad since her mum had left. He was in bed when she entered and didn't even call down. Thea was elated, she was about to become a rich woman, well able to live an independent life. A quick drink of juice from the fridge, then she grabbed her bag and went up to her room. There was work to do.

But Thea was in for a shock. The SD cards were not in the cameras. Unable to believe it or work out how that had happened, she grabbed the bag and tipped the contents onto her bed, frantically searching through the items. No luck. She'd set the cameras up herself and there was no way the cards could have fallen out. Her stomach flipped. Someone had taken them.

Thea stood up, went to the window and stared out into the blackness. This was down to him, the killer, but how? She'd made a real cock-up. This was serious. Somehow, she must have made him aware of what she was doing, and for all she knew he could be out there now, planning to kill her, like he'd killed Dean.

CHAPTER TWENTY-ONE

Day Four

"Smart place, the city nick," Jess said when they pulled into the car park. "Purpose built, no doubt the heating works too. Lucky buggers. I bet this is a palace compared to what we have to work in."

But Harry wasn't impressed. He'd no ambition to work at a high-profile station. Ryebridge was no picnic, but the teams here had the Manchester villainy to deal with. There was no way Harry wanted that. Above all, he wanted to keep a low profile, so the forgotten, old-fashioned backwater of Ryebridge suited him just fine.

"I could easily work here," Jess went on, gazing around as she climbed out of the car. "Bet promotion's a lot easier to get too."

"Be careful what you wish for," Harry warned. "Your next step is DI, and you know what that brings with it." She could do it too, Jess oozed ambition, and she was liked. She was an attractive young woman who got along with almost everyone. If she applied for promotion, she'd be encouraged. No doubt about it.

She smiled at him. "You seem to manage, after a fashion."

But Harry wasn't in the mood. He was concerned about the forthcoming meeting with Weeks. He didn't want to hand the case over, but if the man insisted, and Rodders backed him up, there'd be no option.

"Don't you want to climb the ladder?" Jess asked him.

He shrugged. "One day, perhaps, if I last that long."

"I don't get you, Harry Lennox. At times I wonder what you're doing in the job."

She wasn't alone, but he could hardly tell her the truth, and for the same reason, he couldn't come clean to Isla either.

Superintendent Joe Weeks had them shown up to the main office. The large open-plan space was busy, with about twenty CID officers working away at their desks. On one of the walls there were three incident boards, covered in photos and notes.

Harry went forward to take a closer look. It took him a minute or so to take in what he was seeing. In some respects the boards were similar to Dean's. Nadir Nazir was there, and the man who was on Dean's board with Lana and the faceless man. The middle board had six faces on it, two were from the Galashiels killings. But it was the heading above the boards that made him gasp. Two words that all the officers in the Greater Manchester area had been familiar with for months.

"This is 'Operation Songbird!'" he exclaimed. "Is that what we've stumbled into?"

"That's right," Weeks said from behind him.

Harry should have realised. Songbird was very much the territory of the Manchester force.

Songbird was an investigation into a number of murders that had taken place over the last couple of years. Particulars sent to all the stations stated that the killings were thought to be drug related. Harry had skimmed the updates, particularly the bit about the killings being linked to organised crime and had left it at that. Not for one moment had he considered linking Songbird to their own current case.

"Let's take this somewhere quieter." Weeks led them to a smaller office where a second man was waiting for them.

"This is DI Jack Parkinson," Weeks said. "He's been on Songbird since last year."

Harry smiled in greeting. The DI simply nodded, his expression surly. This obviously wasn't suiting Parkinson any more than it was him.

"We're all hunting a killer who's far too successful for comfort," Weeks began once they'd sat down. "Therefore it's important we share the information we've gathered so far."

"Is that what Songbird is, the search for this killer?" Jess asked.

"Partly, but the operation is rather more complex than that."

This intrigued Harry. As far as he was concerned, their part was simple — they had a killer to catch. What was Weeks looking for out of this?

"Your team are new to the case. You've done well, but there's no sense in you going over groundwork we've already covered. In return, you will share with us your findings so far."

That seemed fair enough, at least Weeks hadn't asked them to hand the case over. Given that Songbird was so high profile, that surprised him.

"I've read some information on Songbird. I'm aware it's thought to be big-time drug dealing run by organised crime. But that's not how I see the case we're working on," Harry said. "So far there hasn't been a hint of anything related to drugs."

"But it is related. You'll see when I tell you what we have so far," Weeks said. "You've asked the usual questions, spoken to the families, and looked for links between the victims. Am I right?"

Harry nodded. "There are links between at least two of the victims — Nadia Nasir and Lana Midani. They're sisters, and we're working on the others."

"And the man, Roebuck," Parkinson said, "because he's also linked to Ms Nasir and possibly her sister."

Harry's eyes narrowed. He didn't recognise the name. "Roebuck? We don't know about him."

"Oh yes, you do," Weeks said. "His photo is up on your board. Fair impressed me that did."

"Is he the man on the same board as Lana and the face-less man?"

"Yes, and like you we reckon they are the killer's next victims."

"We might have his photo but until now we didn't know his name," Harry explained. "And you're sure this Roebuck was known to Nadia and Lana?"

"He was known to Nasir, there is no doubt about that," Weeks said. "Roebuck delivers laundry to the hotel she worked in, the Commodore."

"The two Scottish victims. Where do they fit in?" Harry asked.

"As far as we're aware, they have nothing to do with Nasir or the people the killer is still after. We believe they're a different job but still connected to Songbird."

"The people responsible for the killings operate coun-trywide then?" Jess asked.

"We believe so. The man who killed all the victims you know about has gained himself a fearful reputation, which is why those who run Songbird use him."

"Does he have a name?" Jess asked.

"We don't know who he is, which makes him very use-ful to them. He could be anyone — a neighbour, a busi-nessman, we have no idea." He paused while Harry and Jess took this in.

"We are aware that he knows his stuff. He's giving the forensic team we use a right headache," Jess said.

"That's what I'd expect," Weeks said. "This killer is not a serial killer with some weird motive for what he does. This man is told who to target and he's paid extremely well for getting it right. It's his job, and he's good at it. The man you're after is a paid assassin."

CHAPTER TWENTY-TWO

Harry and Jess looked at each other. The shock sank in.

"We've been on this case for months and have built up quite a body of knowledge," Weeks continued. "We have a shrewd idea who the assassin does most of his work for locally. The Scottish killings took us by surprise. All we know is that they were drug related too, and we're still investigating the connection."

"And you're sure about this?" Harry asked, still getting his head around it.

"Definitely. An assassin who's paid for every hit and is an expert at his craft. The link you're after for the killings has nothing to do with the victims or even the assassin, but rather the man who employs him, and that's where the big-time drug-running comes in. Catching the killer is a priority of course, but it's even more important to get the man at the top."

Parkinson addressed Harry. "You're Scottish, transferred from Glasgow within the last few years. D'you recall any of the villains you dealt with back home who might fit the bill?"

It was logical that he should ask the question. No doubt Parkinson had looked up his history. Nevertheless, the question put Harry on edge, made him wonder exactly what he knew, and who he'd been talking to. He smiled. "The usual motley of dealers and thugs. After a while they all melt into one."

"Not all of them. There's at least one who's very enterprising, runs his own empire," Parkinson said. "We think he is responsible for the Galashiels killings. We don't know much, other than that he's a big-time Glasgow gangster, but we'll have a name soon I'm sure. I had hoped you'd be able to offer us some possibilities."

Harry saw the look on Jess's face. She knew how hard he tried to conceal his Scottish past and she was concerned he'd flip.

"Glasgow villains?" Harry queried evenly. Jess looked surprised. "Perhaps we should leave them to the force up there. They know better than us what's going on."

"True," said Parkinson, "but it was our assassin who carried out the murders. So he has at least one more connection than we thought. The more we know about him the better." Parkinson smiled. "Our colleagues north of the border will share what they know, and we will reciprocate."

A killer on his patch who wasn't averse to doing a Scottish villain's dirty work. That wasn't good. "How d'you know the local killings and those in Scotland are linked?" Harry strongly suspected they were — they had Dean's wall to work with — but it wasn't proven. Yet.

"Good detective work," Parkinson replied, a smug look on his face. "Much the same as how you found out about the next batch of victims. We've cooperated with the Scottish forces, and they've shared certain information about the nature of the deaths."

"What information?" Harry asked. "If it's pertinent to the case, we need to know."

"How the victims were killed, type of knife used, that's all," Weeks said. "He uses the same knife for every kill. Think of it as his trademark if you like. We know the length and width of the blade and that it's double edged."

That was what Melanie had told them. "Okay, who is this local man that does the hiring?" Harry asked.

Parkinson looked at Weeks, who nodded. "He's the biggest distributer of drugs in Greater Manchester."

"Does he have a name, this villain?" Harry persisted.

Weeks had a thick file on the table in front of him. He passed it to Harry. "That's a copy of everything we know. I want you to understand that the information in there wasn't got easily. My team worked tirelessly to assemble it."

Jess eyed the file. "So, why not arrest him? You look to have plenty in there."

Ignoring this, Weeks returned to Harry's question. "We strongly suspect our man is one Ricky Calvert," he paused, "but that's not yet proven." He smiled at Jess. "If it was, we'd have him behind bars, believe me. The problem is finding proof. Calvert is good, he covers his tracks. What we need is someone close to him to talk to us. Unless you are — close to him, that is — you'd never know he was anything other than what he appears to be."

"And what's that?" Jess asked.

"A respectable businessman," Weeks said. "He owns a number of bars and hotels around the area. But what we need is evidence linking him to his other interests. Those are mainly drugs, with moneylending as a side-line. There isn't a dealer in Manchester who could operate without going through Calvert. He is vital to the trade. Ms Nasir worked for Calvert, quite legitimately, in one of his hotels — the Commodore in the city centre. She absconded with a fortune in heroin, hence the vendetta."

"You said Calvert owns hotels," Harry asked. "Is the Metropole one of his?"

Weeks looked at him and raised his eyebrows. "And that's in your neck of the woods."

Dean Greenwood had worked there. That was the link between them. Both Dean and Nadia had worked for Calvert. Nadia's sister, Lana, had stayed in the Metropole. The pieces were coming together. "Nadia was just a young woman waiting on tables, how did she manage to get her hands on the drugs? Did she have help?" asked Harry.

"Yes, we suspect Roebuck, whose photo is among Greenwood's clippings."

"And the attempt on Lana Midani's life?"

"When Nadia was murdered, the heroin was never found," Weeks explained. "We know she rang her sister the day before she died, and no doubt Calvert does too. It's likely he suspects that Lana has the heroin or knows where it is."

Lana had kept that one to herself. "What about Roebuck? What did he do to help?"

"He works for the laundry where the Calvert hotel sends its washing. He is one of the delivery men. We know that Nasir and Roebuck had struck up a friendship. He often gave her a lift home. Roebuck has history and knows people who can sell the drugs on."

"Do you know where Roebuck lives?" Harry asked.

Weeks smiled. "Ryebridge. So you'd better get him found quick and put somewhere safe."

"How did Nadia get her hands on the drugs in the first place? Could that have been down to Roebuck too? Could he be one of the delivery men?" asked Jess.

"We considered that, but no. He's not whiter than white but recently he's been keeping a low profile. We've searched his van more than once, and all we ever found was clean laundry." Weeks chuckled. "We think Nadia Nasir was the person who looked after the deliveries at the Commodore. It makes sense. For reasons we can only guess at, that night she took off on her own — with Calvert's drugs. Calvert won't stand for disloyalty but more important than that, he wants his drugs back."

"Is it possible that she arranged for Roebuck to sell them on for her? Perhaps that's why she cultivated the friendship," Harry said.

"Yes, and we reckon that's exactly what Calvert thinks happened too. Hence, he gets his assassin to take the lot of them out."

"There's a third image on Dean Greenwood's board, a man with no face. Any idea about him?" Harry asked.

"No, he's something of a puzzle. But we're sure he's connected to either Calvert or possibly the Glasgow villain. Unfinished business," Weeks said.

"How could you possibly know that?" Harry asked. "This assassin could be working for someone else entirely. The faceless man may not be connected to any of the victims we know about."

"It's possible, but we have nothing to suggest our assassin works for anyone but Calvert and whoever employed him in Glasgow. No doubt the villain has him on a retainer," Weeks said. "Over the years this killer has got rid of any number of Calvert's enemies. The Scottish angle — the Glaswegian villain — we have no idea about, but it's possible that he and Calvert have some deal in mind."

Harry felt his stomach churn. Any major villain in Glasgow was bound to have a link to his old enemy, Mungo Salton, the last person Harry wanted connected to his patch.

"If this Calvert is such a big-shot villain, why doesn't he have his own killer?" Jess asked. "Why hire in an assassin?"

"Our Mr Calvert has a reputation to maintain, that of a squeaky-clean businessman. He wouldn't want anyone connected with him or his business to be involved in murder. He is careful to ensure that there is no one to give evidence against him."

"Yet he's quite happy to have large consignments of drugs dropped off at his hotels. It doesn't make sense," Jess said.

"That's very well controlled, the Nasir incident apart. He only uses a few trusted people, and the drops are cleverly organised. We have tried to intercept one but so far without success. We know that large amounts of drugs make it to Calvert's hotels but we have no idea how. To date, we haven't been able to get Calvert on anything. He uses the assassin so that he doesn't get his hands dirty," Weeks said.

"We know very little about the Scottish villain other than that he bears grudges," Parkinson piped up. "The force in Glasgow reckon that's what the Galashiels killings were about — getting even. The information we have is that the two victims were working together in an effort to avert an attempted take-over by the big boss up there. We were hoping that you might know a little more about what goes on up there, throw a few names into the pot."

It was the way he'd said it. Harry didn't like the DI's tone. He was making this sound personal, *and it couldn't be.* "You sure you don't already know? You must have a list of possibles."

"So must you, DI Lennox. But the theory of Calvert working with a Glasgow villain needs more research. We'll get back to you," Parkinson said.

"Look, it's not our intention to hold anything back," Weeks said. "We aren't in competition here. We want this killer and the bastard who hires him every bit as much as you do. But it will take work. I suggest you do your bit, and we'll do ours, but there must be cooperation. Each team must keep the other informed of every move."

A nice idea, but Harry had the distinct impression Parkinson wasn't keen, and that he had an agenda of his own. "The others on that board, apart from the Scottish victims and Nadir, are they local?"

"All within the Greater Manchester area and we believe all connected to Calvert in some way. Some of the cases are old, but all were killed using the same method and we believe all by our assassin," Weeks said.

"How can you be so sure this Calvert is the man hiring the assassin?" Jess asked. "D'you have evidence?"

"Our original suspicions about Calvert are based on information we gathered from a disgruntled ex-employee. He'd crossed Calvert and was terrified for his own safety and that of his family. We put him in a safe house in exchange for anything he could tell us. It wasn't much but it led us to believe that Calvert headed up the distribution of drugs and that it was him who hired the assassin."

"Can't this ex-employee give evidence against him?" Harry asked.

"His statement is based on overheard conversations. None were recorded, and there's nothing which will stand up in court."

"Has anyone spoken to Calvert?" Harry asked. "Faced him with what you know?"

"Yes, me," Weeks said. "But he was never going to admit to having people killed. His reaction can best be described as outrage. He had alibis up to his armpits for every single one of the killings, and he denied even knowing Nadia Nasir or the others. Said he couldn't be expected to know every waitress his company employs. Arrogant bastard. And we have no idea how Calvert and his killer make contact. Burner phone is favourite, but then we have the problem of how the phones are passed to the assassin."

"They could be posted to him," Jess suggested.

"That's a possibility."

"Or they could use some anonymous method of communicating. We have a laptop belonging to Dean Greenwood. He knew the assassin, and he didn't find him on the dark web," Harry said.

"So how does finding the assassin lead us to Calvert?" Jess asked.

"That's our job," Weeks said. "Find the assassin and there will be a trail leading back to Calvert, has to be, and we'll follow it."

"What's the betting Calvert lays a trap and has the assassin killed before he has a chance to say anything," Harry said.

"You're right. It's exactly what Calvert would do, and our assassin knows it. You catch him, and in exchange for making him safe, he'll talk. It'd be stupid of him not to."

Weeks had a point. "I wouldn't mind a word with Calvert myself," Harry said. "Get the measure of the man."

Weeks grunted. "Not happening. Leave Calvert to us and concentrate on your side of this case. Check up on Roebuck and keep Ms Midani safely out of the way. Your killer is top of his game and he has a contract to fulfil. He knows the man who hires him will want blood if he fails."

CHAPTER TWENTY-THREE

Meeting over, Harry and Jess returned to their car, stunned by what they'd just learned. They sat in silence for a few minutes.

"Not what I expected to hear," Jess said, eventually.

"Me neither. I genuinely thought Weeks would steal the case from under our noses. Instead, he's given us a lot to think about."

"I hadn't considered it, but given what we know, a paid killer makes sense. But then what do we do about Calvert?" Jess asked.

"Weeks said to leave him, so for now he's his," Harry said.

"And the Scottish villain? Do you have any ideas on that one? You had that weird look on your face when Parkinson asked."

"Like I said, I can't think of anyone in particular. Anyway, we've enough to think about with our own killer, without adding more to the mix. I'm more interested in the fact that Dean and Nadia both worked at hotels owned by Calvert, and Roebuck's job took him there. The Commodore and the Metropole will get a visit." Harry started up and pulled out of the station car park. "Hopefully, we'll find this character Roebuck still alive. I'll get Col on it. He can ring the laundry company and get his address."

"If the killer hasn't got to him first," Jess said. "Though if Roebuck's lucky, the killer will still be looking for Lana. He'll be under pressure from Calvert to get that job done. I hope they're keeping security around her tight and she's playing by the rules."

"We'll pay her a visit on our way back to the station," Harry said. "We can remind her and while we're at it, let her know we've discussed her sister's involvement with the drugs. She needs to talk to us, Jess. That young woman has kept important information back. If she does know where that heroin is, Calvert will go to any length to get it back and that ups the pressure on us all."

"I'll ring Col and get him to look for Roebuck," Jess said. "Lana needs to be a deal more candid with us, be made to understand how serious this is."

"We asked her if she knew who Nadia was working for and she lied to us," Harry said. "She said the man was a loan shark, not a big-time dealer. She knows the danger. I don't understand what she's playing at."

"She doesn't want us getting too close to the truth."

"My thoughts exactly, Jessie. I believe that young woman knows exactly what happened to the heroin and has plans for it."

* * *

Lana was in a safe house some ten miles outside Ryebridge. The location known only by Harry, Jess, the family liaison officer and the two officers posted on guard duty. The FLO let them in. She wasn't smiling.

"I'm sick of being stuck here with that woman," she complained. "Lana seems to think I'm some sort of slave. She can't cook, can't even hang up her own clothes. This one's a right selfish cow and no mistake. She expects me to run around at her beck and call all day long."

"Well, we've got new information. She tells us the truth and you won't be stuck here much longer. We're doing all we can to find the killer and whoever hired him," Harry said. "Meanwhile, like her or not, we must put Lana first and not forget she's in grave danger."

Harry went through to the small sitting room to speak to Lana. Her expression said it all. She was no happier with the current arrangements than the FLO.

She directed her gaze at him, her dark eyes flashing with anger. "How much longer? This is a complete waste of my time. I need to get back to London. I have work, engagements. My followers will wonder where I am."

She looked tired. Her face was drawn and she had dark circles under her eyes. Being locked away like this was really getting to her. "Your followers will have to wait, Lana," Harry said gently. "We're working hard to wrap this up, but we need your help. No more lies or holding back. The time has come for you to tell us the truth about Nadia, and then, perhaps, you'll be able to return to your life."

She lowered her eyes and appeared to be considering this. But he'd spotted a small movement of her left hand. She'd just pushed a thin rectangle behind a cushion.

"Is that a mobile?" he asked sharply. "You do remember what we said about contacting anyone or using social media?"

"You don't understand," she wailed. "I need to be online, it's how I earn a living. I have contracts to fulfil. My followers expect to see me, hear me."

"Give the damn thing here," Harry demanded, holding out his hand. "You have a killer chasing you who is good at his job and is being paid to make sure he leaves you dead! How much of that don't you understand, Lana?"

"Sorry," she said lamely. "I didn't think the odd call or post would matter."

"Well, it does, and while we're at it, why didn't you tell me about the drugs your sister stole?"

That threw her. She stared wide-eyed at Harry. "Because I prefer to forget about it. Nadia made a mistake, she got involved with a bad man. How d'you know about that anyway?"

"Nadia was working in the hotel the drugs went missing from, but you knew that. She stole a fortune in heroin. I also think you know what happened to it."

"You're demented. My sister did no such thing!"

"Yes, she did. That's why she died, and why you're here. It's the reason a killer is chasing you right now. The man that stuff belongs to wants it back and he thinks you can help him with that."

Lana folded her arms, a look of defiance on her face. "That's all wrong. You haven't got the first idea."

"Then tell me. Tell me about the drugs and how Nadia got involved. We're not going to sort this, Lana, unless you're honest with me."

She sighed. "It was a mistake. Nadia saw an opportunity and took it. I don't blame her — working in that hotel was nothing short of slave labour. Nadia was sick of being picked on, of having to work every day until she dropped."

"She took the drugs from the man who delivered them. Why would she do that? Nadia must have realised how dangerous that was," Jess said.

"She was desperate and afraid. Nadia had nothing and no chance of getting away from that place. She couldn't cope anymore, just wanted to get away, disappear. I said I would help, give her money, but she said no. I think she wanted a new life entirely, somewhere far away where she'd never be found. The drugs were her way out."

"Did she have help?"

"There is a man who delivers laundry to the hotel. He offered to help her for a fee. He knew people who would take the drugs to sell on. He promised to get Nadia a good price."

Roebuck. The one the Manchester people had mentioned.

"When Nadia's boss found out, he was angry. He demanded his stuff back. He rang her on her mobile the night she ran off, ranting and raving about what he'd do.

She swore she knew nothing, but he didn't believe her. Then Nadia confessed that she'd already sold the drugs."

"Did she say who to?" Jess asked.

"This man — Roebuck. Shortly after that, she was found dead. My sister wasn't the innocent she appeared to be, Inspector. She mixed with some shady people but still, she didn't deserve to die."

"The heroin was never found. Did she give it to Roebuck, or to you?" Harry asked.

Lana looked annoyed. "Me? No, of course not. I hadn't seen Nadia for weeks."

"Are you sure? You have to tell me the truth."

"We spoke on the phone, that's all. I did not help her, and I have no idea where the drugs are."

Lana looked away towards the window, avoiding Harry's gaze. She was lying.

CHAPTER TWENTY-FOUR

They walked back to the car in silence. "You don't believe her, do you?" Jess said after a while.

"No. I'll lay odds Lana knows exactly where that heroin is. Although why she's hanging on to it is a mystery. She knows full well that Calvert won't stop until he gets it back."

"If she won't talk, there's not a lot we can do."

"At least we know she's not going anywhere. When we get back to the station, find out what she was up to online," Harry said.

Meanwhile, Colin had phoned the laundry company and got an address for Roebuck, but when he went round he found the property had been empty for several months. Back in the office, he trawled through the electoral roll and other council records but found nothing.

"The address the hotel gave me drew a blank," he told them when they got back. "I've done a search and found two people with the name Roebuck in Ryebridge," he said. "One's an elderly woman in a care home, she's no family and neither had her husband. The other's a woman who used to live on the Baxendale but has long since moved away. I'm stumped. I don't know where else to look."

"Living under the radar? Visiting, bunking up on a friend's sofa?" Jess suggested. "He's out there somewhere, has to be. Dean had him on his wall and Weeks knows about him too."

"Keep at it, Col," Harry said.

"How did the meeting at the city nick go?"

"Interesting," Harry told him. "We're now part of the Songbird operation. Heard of that?"

Colin nodded. "It's been mentioned in the odd newsletter. Something to do with drug dealing I believe."

"Indeed, and our victims are involved up to their necks."

"Weeks is happy for us to carry on?" Colin asked.

"He appears to be, although that could change at any time. It depends what we find." Harry knew that if they got close to proving that Calvert was behind the drug dealing, Weeks would step in and claim the glory.

Jess sat at her desk and rang Lana's mobile provider. They promised to email details of what she'd been up to these last few days within the hour. She checked the messages on her desk — Dean's phone data was through too. "Dean Greenwood didn't ring many numbers," she told the others. "I recognise his mother's landline but there's a mobile number he rang a lot."

Colin had a list a names, addresses and phone numbers associated with the case, so he took Jess's list and checked it against his. "Thea Connor," he announced. "He rang her almost every day, sometimes three or four times."

"We need another word with that young lady. She made out that her and Dean weren't that close. Another one who can't stop herself from lying." Harry was getting fed up with this. None of the people they spoke to was telling the truth. If she and Dean were close, why hadn't Thea just said so?

Colin was frustrated and it was getting late. "You get off, Col," he told him. "I won't be long. Do us some tea, that casserole you made yesterday will go down nicely."

As soon as Colin was out of the office, Jess burst into giggles. "He's not your bloody housekeeper you know! *Do us some tea*," she snorted. "And he makes casserole. You're a right pair."

"He's very well organised. Likes to lead an ordered life, which happens to include sorting the meal we'll eat the following day," Harry said. "He's a good cook too, but you're right, he is a bit, well, too organised for me. Living with Col has come as a shock to my system."

"That's because you're a slob, Lennox. I'm just glad you're Col's problem and not mine. There's no way I'd want you anywhere near my new place. I pick up the keys on Friday and move into my new house this weekend. Then it's independence here I come."

"Worked out the finances?" Harry asked. "You know, you were wondering how you'd afford the bills, the mortgage and the like."

"I'm taking your advice and looking for a lodger. I've got a couple of girlfriends in mind. I'm sure one of them will be up for it."

He grinned. "There's always me, Jessie. At a push I could be persuaded."

"I thought we'd just discussed that one. You'd be a nightmare, Harry Lennox. My bright shiny new house wouldn't stay that way for long with you around."

"You're wrong there. I'm as quiet as a mouse and tidy too. Ask Col."

* * *

Colin noticed the youths as he parked his car. Two lads, hoods up, milling around the apartment block he lived in. A second or two later he saw Hugh pull up and briefcase in hand, leave his vehicle and make for the entrance. The youths were watching. As Hugh took the steps up to the door, they dived forward and wrestled him to the ground. Colin was out of his car in a flash and running to his neighbour's aid.

"What the hell are you doing?" he shouted. "Leave him! I'm police."

By now the pair were all over Hugh, punching his face and kicking at his body. Colin didn't hold back. He threw himself into the fray, grabbing one of them by the hair and chucking him off. It gave Hugh the chance he needed to get to his feet. He managed to land a punch before the pair ran off, grabbing Hugh's briefcase as they went.

"Thieving bastards," Hugh said angrily, wiping his face.

"You're bleeding. Looks like a bust lip." Colin handed him a hankie. "You're bruised about the face too. Want to go and get checked out?"

"It's okay, no fuss. I'll tend to myself inside. A stiff whisky and then a shower should do the trick."

"You sure? You hit the floor with a bang. You might have a head injury."

"I'm fine, really. I'm more concerned about the loss of my briefcase."

"I'll report it straight away, both the theft and the assault. Uniform might find it discarded somewhere." His friend had had a narrow escape. If he hadn't been there, they could have done Hugh some serious damage. "Would you recognise them again?"

"Ever the copper, aren't you, Col?" Hugh smiled. "I'll give a statement but I don't recall much — hoodies, gloves and young, that's about it."

CHAPTER TWENTY-FIVE

Jess left the station late, having stayed behind to go through the data from Dean's mobile again. She was looking for anything that would help move the case along, but apart from the frequent calls to Thea, there was nothing. A wasted effort, especially when in a week's time she was moving out of her parents' home and had a million things to do. She was making her way to her car when she heard someone call out to her.

"DS Wilde! Jess? I wonder if I could have a word."

She spun round to see a dark-haired woman hurrying towards her with a friendly smile. Her accent was Scottish, so she had to be the woman who'd come to see Harry.

"You're Harry's friend, aren't you?" Jess said. A chat with this woman might give her answers to some of those questions she had regarding Harry, but did she really have the energy right now? Jess was tired and all she wanted was to get home.

"My name's Isla, and yes I am his friend, although you'd never know it. He's refusing to speak to me."

"We've got a tough case on our hands," Jess explained. "He's preoccupied, that's all."

"No, that's not it," the woman said firmly. "I know him. He may not have told you, but I used to be a DS on the same team as Harry in Glasgow. This man you work with is afraid that if he talks to me I'll guess the truth about him."

"Truth? What truth would that be?" Jess prickled. She was in no mood for an argument with anyone, and anyway, what did this woman hope to get from her?

"The truth about who he is, the truth about his past. Working with someone in our sort of job, you get close, learn a lot about each other. You see, I was engaged to Paul Lennox."

This woman knew things, she probably knew Harry better than her, but when it came down to it, did Jess really want to know? What did it matter anyway? Harry was okay. He was good to work with and he got the job done. If there was some huge secret, perhaps it was better to keep it that way.

"Okay, tell me what you want to say, only I'm not up for a *slag off Harry* session," Jess warned.

Isla gave her a long hard look. "You really haven't worked it out, have you? Surely Sandy Munroe must have told you his theory? Harry's dead."

That said, she spun round and walked off into the night. Seconds later, she stopped and turned back. "And if the man you're working with thinks he can spin this elaborate fairy tale and hide from Salton for ever, he's wrong!"

Jess couldn't process this. "Hang on!" she shouted. "You can't say something like that and just walk away. What proof d'you have?"

Isla stared back at Jess. "I was engaged to Paul. I know him, know the little mannerisms, the marks on his face and the scar on his wrist he got falling when collecting shells with me."

"You're wrong. You base this wild theory on one scar," Jess was surprised. "Harry's hands and arms are covered in scars, the fire, remember. The man I work with is a damn good detective. He knows the job, and he works hard and that's who he is. Paul wasn't like that. Harry told me he was one for the easy life. Believe me, there's nothing easy about what we do." This didn't impress Isla one bit.

"Tell Harry from me that he can't hide for ever. One day Salton will find him and he'll know straight away who the man you work with really is."

"Why?" said Jess. "If you're telling the truth, what possible reason would Paul have for pretending to be his brother?"

"He's trying to save his skin, to disappear and not be found."

"If that was really what he wanted, why continue to work as a detective? Granted Ryebridge is no city nick, but Harry'd be easily found if you were determined. And what would Salton want with Harry anyway? I work with him, he's good at his job. I'd know if he was a fraud."

"True, Paul could be feckless but he's clever," Isla Stewart said. "Harry told his brother a lot about the job. They discussed cases and Paul often came up with good ideas of his own." She paused. "Is what I've told you really so inconceivable?"

"Yes, it is," Jess said decisively. "You see, you've forgotten something. The Harry I know checks out on the police database, both DNA and fingerprint-wise. There is no mistake. This idea you have in your head is sheer fantasy."

"D'you know why he stole his brother's life?" Isla said. Jess shook her head. "Because he's afraid. Salton blames Paul for the death of his son. Paul and Josh Salton had been friends since school. I warned Paul to back off, told him the Salton family was poison, but he took no notice. One night, the pair were out and they both got drunk. Josh owned a sports car and despite all advice, he insisted on driving them home. They were both boozed up to the hilt and Josh was also high on heroin." Isla gave a bitter laugh. "Paul had grown close to the Salton clan. He saw them as a way out of his problems. Paul's house-painting business wasn't going well. He sold his car and anything else he could get his hands on, including my jewellery, to get the stake money together to join Salton in a robbery. He really was a first-class idiot!"

"What happened?" asked Jess.

"On the way home, Josh Salton lost control of the car. It left the road and Josh was killed outright — went through the windscreen. Paul climbed out of the car without a scratch on him."

"What about the police?"

"Paul was a passenger and although he was drunk, he hadn't taken any drugs. Josh Salton got the blame. His father swore to get even with the Lennox family. He believed Paul was entirely responsible for what happened, maintaining that Paul should have stopped Josh, got them a taxi, anything other than let him drive. Paul tried to explain. He still wanted to be part of the robbery, but Salton said no. Paul told Harry about the villain's plans and Salton and his crew were arrested. As is the way with Salton, there was insufficient evidence to send him down for long. The main trail led back to Josh, and he was dead. The robbery never happened, and Josh Salton was branded as being every bit as bad as his father. Salton got a few months and while he was inside, he planned how to deal with the Lennox family."

"Salton's revenge was the house fire and the deaths," Jess said.

"He made an example of Paul's family, simple as that."

"Does Salton believe Paul is dead, or is he deluded enough to think the same as you?"

"At first, he believed that Paul died in the fire with his father, but I have information that he now thinks differently. Paul — or Harry, as you know him — won't speak to me, so I'm begging you to warn him because Salton won't let this drop."

Jess shook her head. "Sorry, I can't accept any of this. What you've told me is sheer nonsense. The man I work with is a CID officer, not a painter and decorator masquerading as one. I know that Harry doesn't want Salton finding him but after what happened, that's understandable." She moved closer to Isla Stewart and looked her straight in the eye. "And he doesn't need you coming here stirring up old memories. Harry's life is complicated enough as it is."

CHAPTER TWENTY-SIX

Day Five

Thea Connor was terrified. She'd lain awake all night thinking about the cameras and decided there was only one explanation. Someone had taken out the SD cards, and that must have been the killer.

Thea's instinct was to flee. But that wouldn't work. Her dad would be on her tail in no time. She might be allowed to come and go as she pleased, but she always had to be home at night. Thea needed an interim plan until she worked something out.

Meanwhile, Thea decided the best thing to do was continue her normal life. Go to school, do her hours at the Metropole. That way, no one would notice anything was wrong, but more important, she'd be with people. The last thing she wanted right now was to be alone.

It was half term and she'd agreed to put in extra hours at the hotel. Agnes Wright had a job in the office she wanted doing. It was usually quiet in there and it would give Thea time to think. She desperately needed a plan.

Thea was a nervous wreck. She felt too sick to eat, and yesterday had done nothing but lie in bed thinking about her predicament. The big question, the one that plagued her most — did he know who she was? Another problem was Roebuck. There'd been nothing on the local news or in the press about a body being found on the Baxendale. That had to mean one thing — Roebuck was still lying where she'd last seen him. Dead on his sitting room floor.

And how could the killer know who she was? She'd been careful, worn dark clothing and pulled her hood down low over her face. Even if she'd been caught on camera, it would be hard to tell if she was even male or female.

Besides, her situation was very different from Dean's. The idiot had made himself known to the killer, been upfront, even agreed to meet him. No, weighing up the odds, she reckoned she was safe. But how to stay that way? Hiding would get her nowhere. Anyway, it wasn't possible. She had a shift at the hotel. Best thing — just get on with it. She'd be with people and her dad would pick her up after work.

She was about to leave the house when her mobile rang. She glanced at the screen — a number she didn't recognise. Thea should have given it more thought, but she didn't. "Yeah?" she said, balancing the phone under her chin while she gathered her things for work.

"You've been meddling in things that don't concern you."

Thea dropped what she'd been holding and pressed the mobile tight against her ear. It was him. Had to be. She heard the menace in his tone. "Sod off," she spat. "Give me any trouble and you'll get twice as much back." Bravado. Thea stood, trembling. This was a vicious killer and she was no match.

"A feisty one, eh? But taking me on is not a good idea. I know what you did, Thea, and I'm watching you."

Her stomach turned over. Was he outside, waiting to strike as she went for the bus? "I know what you did. I'll go to the police, tell them everything."

"Everything?" He laughed. "You have nothing. They won't listen."

"Oh, they will, don't you worry. There's a detective on the case who'll hang onto my every word."

"Ah, the resourceful DI Lennox." He paused for a moment. "I have a better idea, Thea. Let's meet. Discuss terms. That is what you want, isn't it? To blackmail me?"

That had been Dean's idea. Is this what happened to him? Had the killer lured him to a meeting, late at night, in a lonely spot, and then knifed him? "How did you find me?"

"I'm an expert, Thea. You . . . you're a mere kid chancing her luck. I have Dean's mobile. You were practically the only person he called, apart from his mother. You didn't factor that in, did you? Very careless. Shame it has to end this way. I admire you — you took risks, almost got what you wanted. The camera idea was inspired — the images are first class by the way — but you still wouldn't have got me to pay up. I'd have killed you first. On the other hand if you'd taken them to the police, I wouldn't have stood a chance, they'd have recognised me at once."

"Leave me alone. There's no harm done. You're right, I have no proof and no idea who you are."

"What? Didn't Dean tell you?"

"No, he didn't."

"Okay, in that case we'll call this a warning. But interfere in my business again and you'll end up like Dean."

Thea sighed with relief. It looked like he'd seen sense and would let her live. Now she thought she was off the hook, curiosity got the better of her. "How did you know about the cameras?"

"I didn't. Not until I had a fight with Roebuck. He hit me and drew blood. I would have cleaned up straight away — wouldn't want to leave any DNA for the police, that would make things too easy. But the busybody in the flat upstairs was alerted by the noise and started to shout. I left, turned out the lights and returned later when it was quiet again. You obviously didn't see me, the place was in darkness. Luckily for me the camera in the sitting room had been knocked over in the fight. Neat little gadget, full marks to you. I picked it up, realised what it was, removed the SD card and put the camera back where you'd left it. I searched the rest of the house and found the others. Unlucky for you that fight, your plan almost came off. But that's how things work out sometimes."

"Did you see me then, that night?"

"Yes, and I would have taken you out too, but you walked off with those teenagers. If you hadn't, you'd have been found the following morning, dead in a gutter on the Baxendale."

The call ended. Thea stood there for a while. She was scared witless. Was she safe or not? She certainly didn't trust him. She locked the front and back doors and went up to her room. She needed to think. This man was a real threat. For two pins, he'd kill her. She went over their conversation in her head, and then something struck her. He'd said the police would recognise him from the images caught on camera. That meant he was known to them. Perhaps she could use that. One thing was certain, Thea needed this man out of her life for good. Almost an hour and several mugs of coffee later, Thea had worked out a plan of sorts to trap him. It was risky, he was obviously no fool so whatever she said would have to be good. She called him back.

"I have to know where I stand. You killed Dean and you could easily kill me."

"You're right, but there's nothing you can do about it."

"What if there was? What if I could help you in some way, in return for you promising to leave me alone?"

"How?"

"I won't go to the police. I won't tell them what I know." There was no response, so she ploughed on. "You'd be daft to refuse my offer. Dean told me things about the set-up. He said that everything you do is arranged anonymously using a website and burner phones. He also said that you've never met him, this man who hires you to kill. That doesn't seem fair to me." She paused for a moment to let him think about this. "Then there's the danger. Suppose he decides to have a change, hire someone else? You'll be first on the hit list. Is that a risk worth taking? I don't think so."

"You could be right. You're a bright girl, Thea. But he's at just as much risk as me. I could take him out first."

"Dean said you'd never get close."

A longer silence followed. Finally, he said, "I think you and me might strike a deal."

"Good decision. You get peace of mind and I get the money I was after, plus your promise to leave me alone. What d'you say?"

"All the more reason for us to meet."

* * *

Harry looked up from his desk at Jess. "You're very quiet this morning. Not like you at all."

"Headache," she muttered.

"What're you working on?"

"Why Thea got so many calls from Dean but when we asked her, pretended not to know him that well."

Harry shrugged. "Teenagers. I wouldn't even try."

"They worked for the same hotel chain, the one involved in the drugs trade. I want to know more about that, Harry. She's hiding something, you could tell from her attitude, the way she spoke to us about him. She knows something and doesn't want to say. Have you considered that Dean could have found out something while he was working at the Commodore and that's why he was killed? He worked in the office, he was tech savvy, and we know he was nosey as hell."

She could be right. "Okay, find out if Thea is working at the Metropole this morning and we'll pay her a visit. You and the headache up for that?"

"I'll be fine. How's Col doing with his search for Roebuck?"

"Dead end. Right now he and a couple of uniforms are knocking on doors around the Baxendale asking if anyone knows him. A neighbour of the woman with the same name

— the one who moved away — said the family used to live in the house where Roebuck lives now."

Harry got up from his desk and took his jacket from the back of the chair. "Let's hope no one takes on our Col. He oozes 'copper' and that doesn't do on the Baxendale."

"He'll be careful, Col takes no risks and the uniforms will have his back." Jess made the call and was told that Thea was working a shift in the office.

"Thought she might be," Harry said. "It's half term, you see. Right then, the Metropole it is."

"How d'you know it's half term? You haven't got kids," Jess asked.

"As well as lecturing, Hugh has a part-share in a dental practice. This week will be busy with kids and check-ups, so he's working there at the moment," Harry said.

"I'll have to meet this Hugh."

"Come for a drink with us one night," Harry said. "You'll like him, he's a good laugh. Mind you, he looks a bit of mess this morning. A couple of youths tried to mug him when he arrived home last night. He copped a face full of bruises and a cut lip. Luckily, Col was on hand to help out or he might have been badly done over."

"Any idea who they were?" she asked.

"Hugh didn't get much of a look, it all happened too fast."

"CCTV?" she asked. "An apartment block like that must have a good system."

"Depends on what Hugh wants to do, it's his call. They did get away with his briefcase. "

"He got beat up, too. Doesn't he want them hauled in and charged?"

"We spoke this morning and he's not keen. Hugh likes the quiet life, and as I said, it's up to him."

CHAPTER TWENTY-SEVEN

When they arrived at the Metropole, the manageress was behind the reception desk and she didn't look pleased to see them. "Back again? What is it now? You do know that Ms Midani is no longer with us?"

"Thea Connor — is she working today?" Jess asked, getting straight to the point.

"She's in the office updating the customer database."

"Can we go through?" Harry asked. "We'd like a quiet word."

The manageress nodded resignedly.

Thea wasn't alone. There were three others in the main office, all busy at the computers. Thea was by the window, her young face lit up by the screen. The moment she spotted the detectives, she shut her computer down.

"What's up, Thea? Something you shouldn't be looking at?" Harry said.

"Private stuff for work," she said. "We're not allowed to share customer information for data protection reasons. Being police, you'll know all about that."

She was right, but Harry didn't appreciate the smart-arsed attitude, not in someone so young. Jess had been right.

"You'd do well not to forget that we're police, Thea. If I consider it necessary, I'll look at all the records I like."

"Point taken. It's just that the boss gets in a right strop if private stuff about the customers comes out."

"Did Dean ever work here?" Harry asked.

"Sometimes, if we were short staffed. Dean was versatile, he worked at all the Calvert hotels in the area. Why are you so interested anyway?"

"Him being murdered could have something to do with it," Jess said sarcastically. "Despite what you say, Thea, Dean was chasing a killer, it was no fantasy. We think he discovered something a while ago, then followed it up with his own research. Do you know anything about that?"

The girl shrugged. "You know what I think about his theories — rubbish, the lot of them. Dean went to work, did the hours and went off home. There's no mystery. Why ask me anyway?"

"The pair of you were friends, close even."

"You've got that wrong. I told you, we worked together occasionally, met up sometimes, that's all," she said.

"He rang you every day, Thea, sometimes more than once," Jess told her. "If you weren't close, why was that?"

Thea Connor sighed and turned towards the window. "Get off my back, will you? I don't know anything about Dean or why he was killed." Another shrug. "He was unlucky I guess. He should have let it go."

"Let what go?" Harry asked. "Come on, what aren't you telling us?"

"I can't tell you anything because I don't know." Her voice rose. "Dean rang me a lot, he was like that. I dunno, perhaps he fancied me or something."

Apart from Dean's mobile call log, they had nothing to prove her wrong. Dean rarely went out, so the two of them hadn't been seen together.

"You attend Ryebridge Academy, is that right? What year are you in?" Jess asked.

"Final year of A levels. I leave in the summer."

"You're eighteen?" Harry asked and Thea nodded. "If you're lying, it won't go well for you. You're an adult, old enough to know where obstructing a police investigation can get you."

The girl simply rolled her eyes.

Harry had said his piece. The girl wasn't going to tell them anything and they were wasting valuable time. But why? She knew what had happened to Dean and despite her protestations, his instinct told him that Thea Connor knew very well what Dean had been up to. He could only hope that she came to her senses before she suffered the same fate.

CHAPTER TWENTY-EIGHT

The police's visit had rattled Thea. She needed to end her involvement with the assassin and get out. She'd been careless. She should've told Dean to delete her number ages ago, but he'd insisted on sharing what he discovered. Thea reckoned the killer had taken Dean's mobile when he'd killed him, and that's how he'd found her number. Made sense. It had said in the paper that the phone had never been found.

"I'm going home," she told her boss shortly after the detectives had left. "I feel sick, think I ate a dodgy pie yesterday."

The woman didn't look impressed. "If you can't make it tomorrow, let me know. We've got a wedding party in and I need all the bodies I can get."

Thea gave her a nod and left. Her dad would be in his office, she'd go there and do her homework — anything was better than being on her own. She joined the shoppers on Ryebridge High Street and then slipped into her dad's place. She'd no idea if the assassin had followed her or not. But at least she had company here and was safe for a while.

"Going to use the computer," she told him. "Research for an assignment."

"I've got a client coming in soon, so no playing loud music on YouTube, all right?" Thea nodded. "But feel free to answer the phone and take messages."

"No Dianne today?" Dianne was her dad's assistant.

"She's taken some paperwork to the court, she'll be back later."

Thea sat at a computer at the back of the office and tried to get on with her work. She was just starting to relax and get her thoughts in order when her mobile rang. It was him.

"When and where? You choose."

Thea had already decided daytime would be safer. The shopping mall was the busiest place she could think of. There was a seating area outside the café, and there were always plenty of people around. He couldn't hurt her there.

* * *

Colin had spent the morning knocking on doors in one of the blocks on the Baxendale. Not the most pleasant of jobs — mostly he got a mouthful of abuse as soon as he showed his badge. The uniforms had the right idea, they'd both held back out of sight. No one had offered anything helpful and he was thinking of giving up. Until he met Dora Bradshaw. She peered at his badge and asked him in.

"Bloody awful man, that Roebuck. Makes a helluva noise and never apologises. Thinks he has the right to roar and swear whenever the fancy takes him. He lives down there, in the flat under me." She tapped the floor with her foot. "He's a drunk too, down the pub every night he is. I'm not surprised he gets into arguments. The other night there was a right ruck. Banging, shouting . . . I had to knock on the floor and shout down. Things got quieter after that, and I haven't seen him since."

"Has he lived there long?" Colin asked. "I checked all the records and drew a blank. The tenant in that flat is down as being a woman called Enid Hope."

"That's his mother. She left Ryebridge three years ago. She married again when her old man died. Officially it's still her flat — Roebuck pays her the rent, and she passes it on to the council. That way he gets to stay put."

"Is that allowed?"

She laughed. "Who's going to argue with Roebuck? Have you seen the size of him? He's a huge brute of a man and handy with his fists. Anyway, turf him out and no one else is going to want the place. This estate has gone to the dogs. Council aren't daft, they're getting the rent and that's what's important to them."

"And you've not seen or heard him since that night?"

"Not a peep, which suits me just fine." She smiled. "The night he made all the noise, there was a lot of coming and going. His door sticks, you see, to close it you have to pull hard and it tends to bang. I reckon that damn door opened and closed at least three or four times between midnight and the small hours."

Useful information. Colin thanked her and went down to the ground floor to check out the flat for himself. The banging Dora Bradshaw had described didn't sound good. He knocked on the door and getting no answer, peered through the window. He couldn't see much — the blinds were half closed — but he did spot an overturned coffee table. Perhaps there'd been a fight. Colin rang it in to the office. "I'm going inside," he told the PC who answered. "I can't raise Roebuck, and it's possible he's in trouble."

Much to Colin's surprise, the door wasn't locked. He pushed it open and stepped inside. The door from the hallway to the sitting room was open, and he could clearly see a man lying in a pool of blood. Roebuck, had to be. A quick check confirmed he was dead. Colin had to get Melanie Clarke, her team and Harry down here quick.

CHAPTER TWENTY-NINE

Thea bought herself a takeaway coffee from the café and sat on one of the benches by the entrance. The shopping mall was busy, it was raining so people preferred to shop inside. Which suited Thea just fine.

Was she doing the right thing? The question had niggled at her since the killer made contact. Dean had taken this man on and paid the ultimate price. Could she do any better? Dean had maintained there was no danger, said he held all the cards, but he'd ended up dead. Thea sat there, watching the passers-by and pondering her predicament for a good fifteen minutes before a golden-haired cocker spaniel bounded up to her.

"Sorry, he's only a pup and hasn't got the hang of busy places yet, or that he shouldn't talk to strangers." The owner smiled. "Merlin, leave the young lady alone. She doesn't want covering in your hair."

Thea bent down and scratched the puppy's neck. "He's cute."

"An attention-seeker more like," the man said. "And he always makes for anyone he thinks has food."

Thea smiled and held her coffee aloft. "No food, just a drink and you wouldn't like coffee."

The man sat down beside her, placed his overcoat over his knee and lifted the dog onto it. "He'll settle in minute. I've walked him all over town this morning, he should be tired out by now."

The interlude with the dog took her mind off the impending meeting, made things seem almost normal. He'd never dare approach her while she had company. But safe as she felt, that wouldn't get her anywhere. Thea needed an end to this. She checked her mobile. No calls. "I'll have to go."

"Boyfriend?" the man asked. "Stood you up, has he? Attractive young woman like you. I wouldn't stand for it."

"Nothing like that, but it doesn't matter now." She picked up her bag and was about to get to her feet when she felt something hard press into her side.

"Not so fast, young lady. I have a blade poised and ready to strike. Time for you and I to have that talk. Convince me you can be trusted and I might let you live."

It was him! Why hadn't she realised? His easy manner, the dog, it all appeared so natural. He'd had her completely taken in. "Is the dog even yours?" she asked.

"A colleague's."

"There are more of you?"

He smiled. "Just me, and that's more than enough. In fact, I could be your worst nightmare."

"Look, I'm here," she said. "There's no need to threaten me. I've deliberately chosen a CCTV blind spot, and a place where no one will give us a second glance. I want to do a deal."

"Go on then. Now's your chance. Convince me to let you live."

"As I said before, you'll have my silence. I go to the police and life will get tricky for you." Thea waited for a response but he remained impassive. "I doubt that would please your boss either. He's a vengeful man. He'd turn on you."

"Conjecture. Besides, that won't happen." He sat looking away from her, absent-mindedly stroking the dog.

"Do you want to take that risk though? He gets to know about me and Dean discovering you and it'll change everything. I go to the police and he won't risk keeping you on, or even keeping you alive." Thea watched his expression change to one of annoyance. "Have you ever actually met him?"

"No, there's never been a need to conduct our business face to face."

"But he's ruthless, right? He'll have power and influence. A man like that makes a dangerous enemy."

The killer said nothing.

"Look, there's no need for me to speak to the police or anyone else. I promise to stay quiet about what I know, and in return you'll give me ten grand."

He burst out laughing and shook his head. "You really don't get it, do you, Thea? Right now I hold all the cards. In case you hadn't noticed, it's me holding a blade against your body, not the other way around. You're in no position to make any deal. Nothing you have said convinces me that you know anything that would interest the police. They dismissed Dean's ramblings and it'll be just the same with you."

Thea swallowed, turned, and looked him in the face. She was way out of her comfort zone but she'd started this and had to see it through. "You're not listening. I can do you real harm. Pass evidence onto the police, or even worse, tell your boss how careless you've been." She was bluffing. She had no idea who his boss was, but he didn't need to know that.

"You wouldn't dare."

"Oh I would, and I will. Get that knife away from me or I'll shout out and draw a crowd. You don't want that, do you?"

"Exactly what evidence do you have?" he asked sharply. She felt the pressure of the blade ease as it was withdrawn. "Don't you realise how dangerous it is to lie or to threaten me?"

"I know your username." He turned to her with a look of surprise. "You and your boss aren't the only ones who know about that selling website. There's others have figured out what it's used for. And I can describe you," she said. "Kill me and arrangements have been made to send that proof to the police."

He raised his eyebrows. "You're a clever girl, Thea, I'll give you that. Brave too, taking me on like this, knowing what I'm capable of. But what you say is hardly proof. We only go by our usernames, and nothing can be traced back to me or the boss. When you weigh it up, you've got a big fat nothing." He continued stroking the dog. To the casual passer-by, they wouldn't merit a second glance. A man and his dog, chatting to a young woman who'd taken an interest. "Dean tried blackmail, but then you know that. What you perhaps don't know is that during his nosing around, he rattled one cage too many."

That sparked Thea's interest. "What d'you mean?"

"Dean himself became a target. The man I work for saw him as a threat — not to me, to himself and wanted him taking out. It's only a matter of time before the same happens to you, Thea."

"No, that won't happen," she protested. His revelation had thrown her. If she became one of his paid targets, there'd be no hope of bargaining with him. "Anyway, you're wrong, the police have ways of finding out who's used what websites. I tell them what I know, the police will find it interesting and it'll help them find you." She watched his face carefully.

"Okay," he said after a while, "suppose I do agree to pay you, there's no way you're getting ten grand."

"All right. Five then," Thea said. "Agree and we can end this."

"It had better be all right. It's all you're going to get." Again, she felt the blade pressed into her side. "One shove, young lady, and you're badly injured, but the second strike will be right into your heart."

There was a pause. Thea's heart was racing. He wasn't joking. She could feel the tip of the blade, digging in. "How do we do this?"

"Meet me here tomorrow afternoon, same time and place, and bring whatever you've got with you. It checks out, I'll hand over the cash."

"And then you'll leave me alone?" Her voice was shaking. The man had a knife and Thea knew he wouldn't hesitate.

"Of course. We've made a deal, haven't we?"

CHAPTER THIRTY

"How long has he been dead?" Harry asked as soon as Melanie appeared in the doorway of Roebuck's flat.

Pulling the mask from her face, she said, "You're all the same, demanding instant answers you know I can't give you. I'd say no longer than forty-eight hours, but I'll only be certain after the PM. Like the others, a stab wound to the heart killed him, but there is more this time. The place is a right mess. Judging from the overturned furniture, I reckon they had a fight. There are grazes and bruising to Roebuck's knuckles, so he must have done his attacker some damage. There is plenty of blood. If we're lucky, and he didn't wear gloves, we might get a trace of the killer's blood too. But the scene will take time to process, so you'll just have to be patient, Harry."

"A fight. That's a departure from the norm. Anything else?"

Melanie nodded. "There's blood all over the floor and plenty of footprints. I reckon one set belongs to our killer. I'll check, but it looks to me like the same tread as at the boating lake. Then there's another set, a smaller foot, trainers I'd say."

"There was someone else here?"

"I'd say so," Melanie said. "Whether that person witnessed the killing is another matter. They may have come inside after Roebuck had been killed and stood in the blood. See," she pointed, "the prints lead outside, there's faint marks on the concrete there."

"I wonder if anything is missing. Someone sees an opportunity and robs the man as he lies dead."

"We have no proof of that. But we'll give the flat a thorough going over, take swabs, look for any evidence."

Harry nodded. Melanie was good at her job. If there were any clues here, she'd find them.

"Shame we didn't find him sooner," Jess said as they went back to the car.

"We didn't know who we were looking for," Harry said.

"Lana is safe, Roebuck is dead, that just leaves the faceless man. What do we do about him?"

"How can we do anything?" Harry asked. "We have nothing to go on. He could be anyone."

"Well, he's either connected to Calvert or that Scottish villain Weeks was going on about," Jess said.

"I hope not."

"I spoke to Isla Stewart last night," Jess said. "She collared me when I was about to go home."

Harry sighed. This was what he'd been afraid of, Isla filling his partner's head with rubbish. "What did she tell you?"

"About the car crash, Josh Salton's death and plans for the robbery. She said that's why the villain is after you — she believes the passenger in that car was you, not your twin. She also said Salton reckons whoever was in that car should not have let Josh drive that night, shouldn't have walked away after the crash, leaving him to die."

"She's wrong, about all of it. I discussed it with Paul. There wasn't anything he could've done. Josh Salton was an idiot, but a dangerous one — cross him, stop him having his own way and he'd do you serious harm. That night Josh was bladdered and full of heroin. Mungo Salton refuses to see what's staring him in the face — that his son was just no good. Mind you, Paul wasn't much better either. No way should he have thrown in his lot with Salton and then gone to the police. That was just asking for trouble. I don't know where Isla got hold of the idea that I'm Paul but she's wasting her time."

"I agree, and I told her I didn't believe a word of it." Jess took his arm and squeezed it. "You're a good detective, Harry Lennox. There's no way you're really a painter and decorator, it makes no sense. Anyway, everything about you on the database checks out. I told her that too."

Harry was surprised. So, finally, he'd turned Jess around and she was on his side. "Thanks. I appreciate your support. Did Isla say whether she was going home?"

"No, and I didn't ask. To be honest, the woman annoyed me. I don't know what she hopes to gain by trying to tarnish your name like this."

"Perhaps Salton has paid her to find me. Or maybe he threatened her. Yeah, that would make sense."

"Be careful, Harry. We're up against one vicious killer already, without adding another to the mix."

He grinned. "Don't worry about me. I'm used to dodging Salton."

"Col did well today, finding Roebuck," she said, changing the subject.

"He's turning out to be an asset to our little team. But I'm not sure I can continue living at his for much longer. I'm thinking of taking your advice and looking for a place of my own."

"Finally seen sense, eh? A good decision. Tomorrow I'll fill you in about areas to avoid and all that. There are still a few houses left in the development my new place is on. We could be neighbours."

CHAPTER THIRTY-ONE

Day Six

The following day, Brian Isherwood caught up with Harry just as he was going into the station. "I've got the photos you wanted," he said, holding out an envelope.

There had been so much going on that Harry had forgotten about them.

"I've put them all on a SD disk — the ones from me, June and Maggie."

Harry glanced at him and noticed the cuts and scratches. "What happened to your face? You look as if you've been in a fight."

Isherwood laughed. "Nothing like that. I was walking the dog on the bridlepath yesterday and fell down an embankment. Missed my footing and rolled all the way to the fence at the bottom. I'm lucky I got away with this little lot. Could have been worse."

Harry recalled Melanie saying she thought Roebuck had tackled his killer and they had fought. Now Isherwood turns up looking the part. "Could I have a word while you're here, please? I've got a few more questions."

"Look, I was on my way to work. I just popped in to give you the disk."

"I won't keep you long," Harry said.

A quick word with the desk sergeant and Isherwood was shown to an interview room to wait. "Give him a coffee, keep him sweet — I won't be long."

Harry bounded up the stairs to the first floor and the main office. He passed the envelope with the disk to Colin. "Check those out, Col, they're Isherwood's photos. If you find anything interesting, I'm with him in interview room one."

"Why?" asked Jess.

"Because his face is covered in fresh scratches. He told me he fell down an embankment when he was walking the dog, but he could have been in a fight. I'm thinking Roebuck. Jess, you can join me."

The phone rang while Harry was talking to Jess. Colin, who had taken the call, turned to the two of them. "That was Hettie. They found a bottle of expensive whisky in Roebuck's sitting room. It was still in the box and appeared to be unopened. She says it's been drugged — a tranquilliser. She reckons there was enough there to knock him out for hours."

Harry looked at Jess. "That's a departure from his usual method. I wonder what made him do it."

"Roebuck was a big bloke. Perhaps the killer thought he needed an advantage," she said.

"His neighbour said Roebuck was handy with his fists," Col added. "Our assassin didn't fancy the odds so he shortened them."

"She's texted me some pictures. Looks expensive, that whisky. Find out the brand, Col, then see if you can trace where it came from and who it was sold to. But since we've got Isherwood downstairs, prioritise the photos — see if there's anything I need to ask him about."

* * *

Isherwood was pacing the interview room, looking annoyed. "Well? Why am I here, Inspector? I do have a job to go to, you know."

Harry smiled at him. "We'll try not to keep you. I believe you know my colleague, DS Wilde?"

"Just get on with it," Isherwood snapped.

"Fine. Where were you the night before last?"

Isherwood slumped onto a seat. "Why? What does it matter?"

"Just answer the question," Harry said.

"Maggie had a bad day, so June spent most of her time with her. When I returned from work, I made us all some tea and sorted out the photos I've just given you. It cheered Maggie up a bit, she actually smiled at some of them. It was gone midnight before me and Maggie went home."

"And you didn't go out again?" Harry asked.

"It was dark, cold, and anyway where would I go at that time of night?" His tone had a distinct edge. "Look, it's gone nine. You said this wouldn't take long and now I'm late for work."

"Those marks on your face, tell me again how you got them," Harry said.

"I fell down the bloody embankment on the bridlepath."

"Where on the bridlepath exactly?" Harry said.

"By the bowling green. It's steep just there. The dog had disappeared into the undergrowth and I slipped looking for him. I tumbled most of the way. Want to see the bruises on my shins too?"

There was a knock on the door. Col. Jess went to see what he'd got.

"There's dozens of photos," Col whispered. "It'll take ages to do them justice but nothing's jumped out yet."

"Okay, I'll tell him."

Jess returned to her seat. "Col needs more time," she told Harry.

"Right, Mr Isherwood, that'll do for now," Harry said, "but I will want to talk to you again. Don't take any holidays without checking with me first."

His face like thunder, Brian Isherwood got up from his chair and made for the door. "This is bloody harassment. I intend to complain. You've hounded me since day one. You've got this totally wrong, there's no way I'd have harmed Dean."

They waited until he'd stormed off down the corridor.

"What d'you think?" Harry asked.

"There's plenty about him and his situation that fits the bill, but we've got nothing concrete," Jess said.

"Let's take a wander up that bridlepath, see if there's any evidence of someone falling," Harry suggested.

"You really don't like the man, do you?"

"It's not a question of liking, Jess. But it's clutching at straws time. Unless Hettie or Melanie come up with something from Roebuck's flat, straws are all we've got."

CHAPTER THIRTY-TWO

The whisky was a single malt from a distillery in the Highlands. Colin spent the next hour on the phone ringing all the off-licences and pubs in Ryebridge, asking if they stocked it. But there was no guarantee the killer had bought it locally. For all he knew, the man could have been to the distillery in Scotland and bought it there or even bought it online.

But he was in luck. A shop in the indoor market told him they sold it. Ryebridge market hall had been given a facelift in recent times, the idea being to attract more businesses and shoppers to the area. The Victorian building had been divided out into what the developers hoped would become specialist shops and in the main, that's what had happened. 'Highland Fare' was one of these. It had only been trading for a few months and wasn't yet that well known. The owner, Ray McDonald, said he was happy to see Colin that morning.

Hettie was still processing the bottle itself and its contents, but Colin had a selection of photos of it on his mobile, which he'd printed out in readiness. He was hoping Ray McDonald would be able to tell him who he'd sold it to.

The market hall had just opened when Colin went to look for 'Highland Fare'. He gazed at the freshly painted ironwork pillars holding up the roof. "It's a lovely building. I wasn't even aware the place existed."

"We're doing our best to advertise it and drag in trade from the surrounding areas," Ray McDonald said. "We mostly sell the more expensive end, and folk round here are generally broke."

Colin set out the photos on the counter. "D'you recall selling a bottle of this recently?"

McDonald took an account book from a shelf under the counter and studied it. "That is one I sell. I acquired two bottles on a trip to the Highlands last year. One was bought by Councillor Jones at Christmas — likes his whisky that one, I reckon he's tried every malt we have. The other . . ." Ray McDonald looked up at his shelves. "It's not up there but I can't find a record of it being sold."

"That would be useful," said Colin.

"I jot down the date, too. That particular malt is special. I need to know if a brand sells and if it's worth ordering more. The one you're interested in cost me over fifty quid to buy."

"D'you employ anyone else?" Colin asked.

"Can't afford to."

"Could a bottle have been stolen?"

But McDonald wasn't listening, he was busy flicking through his account book. "I've found it," he said, reading the entry. "One bottle, a week ago." He thought for a moment or two. "He was a well-dressed chap, not local, that's all I can recall I'm afraid."

Colin was fed up with getting nowhere at every turn. "Mr McDonald, this is a murder investigation. A bottle of this brand of whisky was found at the scene and it could have come from your shop. Please, rack your brains. We could do with a more detailed description."

"Look, I get busy in here. I can't be expected to remember every customer."

Colin was pissed off. This case was one dead end after another. "We'll need your fingerprints. There's every chance that if the whisky did come from here, yours are also on the bottle."

* * *

"How far to the bowling club?" Harry asked.

"Round this bend and take the left-hand path. Exactly what d'you expect to find?" Jess asked.

"Something to suggest Isherwood had the fall he claims he had. He's everywhere in this case — Scotland, he knew Dean, he was friendly with the family. We know Roebuck fought with his killer and now Isherwood is covered in cuts to his face. You can't blame me for being suspicious. Right now, the man is a strong contender."

"He doesn't seem the type to me," Jess said.

"What type does an assassin have to be?" Harry said.

"Isherwood strikes me as liking the comfortable, settled life," Jess said. "Bet our killer doesn't live like that. He'll be a loner, go missing for days on end and he won't interact much with the people who live around him."

Harry chuckled. "Quite the little psychologist, aren't you?"

Jess pointed to a large wooden building with a veranda. "There you are — Ryebridge bowling club."

The two of them stood looking down a steep grassy slope to the barbed wire fence at the bottom.

"Do yourself some harm falling down there," Harry said.

"And he did, according to what he told us," Jess said. "And look, the grass is flat over there and smeared with mud."

Harry half-slithered down the slope to a small tree, where he grasped the trunk to steady himself. "There's blood here," he shouted back. "On these blades of grass. There's some thorny branches on this tree. If someone did slip, they could easy get caught up in them."

145

Harry plucked a few blades of grass and put them in an evidence bag. "I'll get Hettie to run some tests, see if it's a match for Isherwood's DNA."

"And if it is, what then?"

"Unless our friends at the Reid come up with something else, Jessie, we're back to square one."

CHAPTER THIRTY-THREE

Thea Connor couldn't believe how involved she'd got. She'd met with a killer and he'd threatened her, held a knife to her body the entire time they'd spoken. As if that wasn't dangerous enough, she, Thea, was blackmailing the man, and actually demanding that he pay over money in exchange for her silence. Given what she knew, how stupid was that!

It had seemed so easy in the beginning. Dean was the one dealing with him, he was going to blackmail the killer and get him to pay over a fortune. He'd agreed to share it with her, and Thea had become a willing accomplice. She thought Dean had died because he was careless and that it was his own fault. Not anymore. He'd been stupid to take on the killer, and so had she. The problem now — how to stay alive.

Thea knew that if she went ahead and met the killer as arranged, he wasn't going to let her walk away this time. Despite agreeing to her terms, he wouldn't risk her talking. This man was no amateur, he'd take what evidence she had to offer, weigh up the risks and leave her dead on that bench. Thea had to do something, get herself out of this mess, but how? She picked up her mobile and found her dad's number. For the first time in as long as she could remember, she needed his help.

"I've got myself in a fix," she began. "I need to talk to you, now, this morning. Can you come home?"

He hesitated before replying, not a good sign. "I've got clients to see, Thea. You know clients, they pay the bills. I can't just rearrange my day to suit you. What is it now — not done your homework? Problem with some boy?"

Just like him. He never had any time for her, his clients always came first. "Nothing like that. I'm in trouble, dad, serious trouble."

"Bloody hell, Thea, you're not pregnant, are you? Anything else I can cope with, but not that."

Thea finished the call. What was the use? Her dad wasn't going to help. She was on her own, so if she wanted to live, there was just one choice left. She took the stolen burner phone Dean had given to her for safe-keeping, plus his third laptop and put them into her school bag. Decision made. She would speak to the police, tell them what she knew and hand over the evidence in exchange for keeping her safe. But she daren't risk going to them — for all she knew the killer was watching her house.

She remembered the card DI Lennox had given her. She took it from her dressing table and keyed in the number, tapping her foot. It was several seconds before he answered.

"It's Thea Connor. I need you to come to my house and get me. I'm in danger and I need your help."

* * *

Harry Lennox put his mobile back in his jacket pocket. "That was a cry for help from Thea Connor. She wants us to pick her up, reckons she's in danger. Any ideas?"

"We suspected she knew a lot more about Dean and what he was up to than she was letting on, that has to be at the bottom of it," Jess said.

"I hope she hasn't attracted the killer's attention and he gets to her before us — that's all we need," Harry said.

"What d'you intend to do?" Jess asked.

He shrugged. "Bring her in."

It took only ten minutes to reach the semi where Thea lived with her dad. Harry could see her watching for them from an upstairs window. "Stay in the car, Jess, and keep your eyes peeled. I'll go and get her."

By the time he reached the front door, Thea was waiting behind it with her stuff. "Thanks. I wasn't sure you'd come. I've been a stupid fool," she said, picking up her bag. "I didn't think I'd feel so scared, but I am, I'm bloody terrified. That lunatic wants to kill me."

"Calm down," he said. "Whatever it is, we'll sort it." Harry escorted her to the car and sat in the back with her. "Let's go, Jess. What's in the bag, Thea?"

Thea opened it up and took out the laptop. "Sorry, I know you've been looking for this, but Dean gave it to me for safe-keeping. And there's this too." She showed him the mobile. "He nicked it from the boss's office at the Commodore."

Harry held onto the laptop and dropped the phone into an evidence bag. Was this where Dean had got his information from? Could it be one of Calvert's burner phones? He held the bag up. "We know the laptop might prove helpful, but where does this figure?"

"It's how Dean's boss sometimes contacted the killer."

If she was right, this could be the breakthrough they needed. Besides the calls, it was possible they'd find Calvert's prints on it.

"I don't know what's on the mobile," she said. "I never turned it on in case it was traced. But Dean reckoned it was important."

"This boss, d'you mean Ricky Calvert?" Harry said.

"Yes, that's what Dean said. Calvert owns the Calvert hotel group, which includes the Commodore and the Metropole in Ryebridge. Dean worked at the Commodore in Manchester which is where Calvert has his main office."

"Why help us now, Thea? When you were questioned before, you said you knew nothing about the laptop, and you didn't attach much credibility to Dean's findings either. Why so scared now?"

"I met the killer," she said softly.

Her admission shocked Harry. What was the girl playing at? That's exactly what Dean had done, and she knew perfectly well what had happened to him. "Where?"

"In the mall, yesterday. All along, Dean had planned to blackmail him, so I thought I'd take over where he left off. The killer would pay me and in exchange he'd get the laptop and the phone, and I wouldn't tell you lot what I know."

"And what do you know?" Harry said.

"That the entire operation is carried out in secrecy, mostly online. Calvert uses the code name 'Songbird' when he contacts the assassin about a kill."

Jesus. Dean really had been busy. "Does the killer know the person who hires him?"

"Yes, but they've never met. For obvious reasons they keep their distance from each other."

"Makes sense," Harry said. "The man who hires him is ensuring his own safety too. He doesn't want to end up a victim."

"Nor does the killer. Dean reckoned Calvert won't let him live once he's finished with him. Thinks he'll hire someone else and the current killer will become his first victim. I thought that would give me an edge, something for him to think about. I was wrong. Now I've seen him, I know he'll just take what I've got and kill me anyway." Thea started to cry. "I can't believe I actually met him. He had a knife, he had it pressed into my side the entire time. But he seemed so ordinary, he even had a dog with him. You'd never suspect he was a killer."

CHAPTER THIRTY-FOUR

"I want Sasha Steele to process these straight away," Harry said to Col. "Take them to the Reid and don't hand them over to anyone but her."

"Thea Connor took some risk. Fancy meeting a killer who you know murdered your friend and then having the cheek to ask him for money." Jess snorted. "Is the girl mad?"

"She got greedy and completely underestimated the risks," Harry said. "Her and Dean seem to have treated this like some sort of game."

"Given what Calvert was hiring the killer to do, would he be so careless as to leave a used burner phone in his desk drawer? Seems a bit far-fetched to me. This man is a seasoned villain who runs an empire, that's not how I'd expect him to behave."

"Perhaps he thought he was safe. He's the boss, it was his office. He has a reputation as a hard man, so who would dare steal from him? Besides, who would know what those phones were for? He considered himself untouchable, Jessie, and that was his mistake."

"D'you think Thea will be honest with us?" Jess asked.

"I don't think she has any choice now. The girl's terrified. We'll interview her, then find her a safe house until this is over."

"What about Weeks?" Jess asked.

"What about him? This is our call. Thea is our witness. We'll tell Weeks what we've got when we've worked out how to use Thea's statement and seen what the mobile and the missing laptop give us."

* * *

Thea Connor was waiting in an interview room with a woman officer. She gave Harry and Jess a half-hearted smile. "I owe you an apology," she said. "I've been a fool, I know."

"You're here now, Thea, and that's all that matters," Harry said. "D'you want a solicitor? Perhaps you'd like your dad to be with you."

"Huh. My dad, the solicitor who doesn't give a damn." She looked down. "I asked him for help earlier and he made some excuse about work. I'd told him I was in trouble."

"Perhaps he didn't understand what was wrong, or how really scared you were," Jess said.

"Wouldn't matter if he did. Work comes first with him, it always has."

"I can ring him if you wish," Harry offered. "If I explain the situation, I'm sure he'll want to be here with you."

Thea had tears in her eyes. She nodded and took a hankie from her pocket. "Tell him I need him here — and not to be angry."

Harry left the room to make the call, leaving Jess to deal with the tearful girl.

* * *

"It must be hard for your dad," Jess said. "I believe there's just the pair of you, isn't there? Not easy, particularly when your dad is running a business."

"Don't make excuses for him," Thea retorted. "He doesn't deserve it. I hate him for letting me down this morning. I don't ask for much, but the one time I really need him to be there for me, he refuses. He puts his bloody clients first." She looked down. "That's why me and Dean got on, we had a lot in common."

The comment surprised Jess. "His mum gave me the impression that he was the light of her life."

"Sometimes. When it suited her. That woman is a nervous wreck. She's always ill. Some days she doesn't even get out of bed. Dean practically looked after himself. She never bothered much about where he was or if he stayed out late."

"He was eighteen," Jess reminded her.

"Even so, being a parent doesn't just stop when you come of age."

Jess nodded. The girl was right. Two teenagers, given all the freedom they want. So what happens? They concoct wild theories and get themselves into a shed load of trouble.

"You should have spoken to us before, Thea."

She sniffed. "I know, don't go on. But I thought I could handle it."

* * *

Harry returned with a mug of coffee and biscuits for Thea. "Your dad is on his way. He did sound worried when I explained what this was about."

"Thanks." She gave him a smile, and then said to Jess, "You're right. If I'd come to you before, perhaps Dean wouldn't have died."

"You knew what he was doing?" Harry asked.

"Yes. I was waiting for him to ring me that night. He said he would, and he'd tell me how it went."

"And when he didn't?"

Thea shrugged. "I fell asleep. I never for a minute thought that Dean would come to any harm. It all seemed so cut and dried."

CHAPTER THIRTY-FIVE

Thea's dad, Rob Connor, arrived within ten minutes of Harry's phone call.

As soon as he walked in, he started to berate his daughter. "For heaven's sake, Thea, why didn't you tell me what was going on? You should have made it clear this morning how serious this is."

"I thought I had," she said. "But you'd already made up your mind that it wasn't important."

But Harry saw the look on the man's face. Thea's dad wasn't angry, he was worried. His daughter had got herself in too deep this time — people were dead, one of them a good friend of hers. He sat down and looked at Harry.

"How did Dean first become aware of what was going on, that there was a killer at work?" Harry began.

"It began when he argued with Ricky Calvert," Thea said.

"What about, d'you know?"

"Work hours. They had Dean down to work a run of six weekends on the trot. He objected, and since Calvert was in that day, Dean took his complaint to the top. Calvert just laughed, said if he wanted the job he'd do as he was told. This made Dean angry. When he saw me later, he said no one could legally make all the money Calvert did. I think he was jealous. Calvert had come to work in a fancy sports car and had been showing round a brochure for a house he was about to buy. Dean had made some sarky comment, and Calvert called him a stupid kid. I think that's what finally did it. A couple of weeks after the argument, Calvert went off to his villa in Greece, so Dean took the opportunity to poke around. He was convinced Calvert was up to no good. He began by hacking into the computer on his desk. It's a standalone, not connected to the hotel system. Dean read Calvert's emails and other stuff."

"What about security? Didn't anybody pick up on what he was doing?" Jess asked.

"No. No one else ever went near Calvert's desk. Even if anyone had noticed Dean, they wouldn't have thought anything of it. If there was ever any problem with the hotel system, they called on Dean. He was brilliant with IT, there wasn't much he couldn't fix."

"Did he find anything?" Harry asked.

"He copied a load of emails and Calvert's browser history. They're on the laptop I gave you."

"And the mobile phone?"

"Dean said there were about a dozen of them in Calvert's drawer. He reckoned they were burner phones — they're all old models. Proof, he said, that Calvert was up to his neck in some scam or other. Dean suspected drugs. He said there were so many phones that one wouldn't be missed. He looked at them all and chose the most recently used one."

"Why did Dean suspect Calvert was into drugs? Had he seen something?"

Thea looked away, shaking her head. "I don't know."

Her voice wavered. Harry suspected she was lying.

"The faces and names on Dean's bedroom wall, where did they come from?"

"The mobiles weren't much use on that score, all that one gives you is a number Calvert called regularly. Dean reckoned it was the killer's."

Harry realised what the lad had done. "Dean rang him, made himself known."

"Yes. By then Dean had worked out what was going on."

"And he was after money?" Harry asked.

"Yes, but it was more than that with Dean. He wanted to show Calvert that he'd sussed him out. I think he'd have pressured both the killer and Calvert for money."

Harry shook his head. "He was playing a very dangerous game. Back to the names and faces, Thea. Where did they come from?"

"The names and locations are hidden in some sort of code Calvert and the killer use. Dean found a website in Calvert's history. He told me the man was never off it."

Suddenly Harry twigged. "The buying-and-selling site?"

"Yes." She smiled. "He didn't tell me how he'd figured it out, or how to decipher the code, but he'll have made notes on his laptop. He got the names on those boards from the information he gathered. Any other information Dean needed about the victims he found in the press or social media."

It made sense. This was the most promising lead they'd had yet, but they still needed to wait for Sasha to check out both the laptop and the mobile. "The entire operation was conducted using the website and some sort of code?" he asked.

She nodded. "Dean tried to get enough evidence to blackmail the killer with. He contacted the site and asked them to tell him who'd placed the ads. He wanted to nail them both. But the site is totally anonymous. Buyers and sellers have usernames and since he only ever places ads and never actually buys or sells anything, there's no trail leading back to Calvert. All the information he used to register with was false — email, name and address, the lot."

"Tell me again what happened when you met him, Thea." Harry said.

"He called and we met in the shopping mall. He seemed perfectly ordinary, friendly even. The dog was cute. He said he'd spent the morning walking him, but that could be a lie. I realised later that the dog was a cover. He agreed to my demands and said he'd pay me to stay quiet. I was tempted, but when I thought about it later, he'd said exactly the same thing to Dean. I realised I'd made a huge mistake and that I had to get out. I knew too much, so he'd have to get rid of me."

"What did you intend to use to blackmail the killer with, Thea?" Harry asked.

She looked at her father and then at Harry. "Just the stuff I know, about him and Calvert. And I'm sorry about that man. I never meant for him to die. I should have come to you sooner, stopped it."

"What d'you mean? How could you have done that?" Harry asked.

"Me and Dean knew Roebuck's name and where he lived. The details about the victims on the site include a date, and Roebuck's do too, so I knew when it would happen."

Harry struggled to hide how angry her words made him. This girl had known Roebuck would be killed and had let it happen to suit her own ends. He wanted to tell Thea Connor exactly what he thought of her but he held back. If he spoke his mind the girl might clam up, and they'd not finished with her yet. He'd submit a report to the CPS and leave it to them. "What did you do?"

"Dean had some spy cameras, they look like air fresheners. I set them up in the flat, and then I went back to collect them after he was dead."

Harry recalled the third set of footprints in Roebuck's blood. They had to be Thea's.

"But the plan didn't work," she said. "The SD discs had been removed. The killer knocked one over and found them."

"You deliberately let that man die, Thea," Harry said.

"Will I be punished? Go to jail?"

Harry didn't want to get into that one. He saw the worried look on her father's face. He knew the law and the ramifications of what she'd done. "That's not for me to say." Thea was crying again, and he decided she'd had enough. "Thanks, Thea, you've given us some very helpful information, but we'll finish for today. You look tired. We'll put you and your dad somewhere safe, well away from Ryebridge, so you can rest."

Rob Connor jumped to his feet. "I can't just walk away from the office. Surely no one's going to come after me?"

"We can't be certain of that," Harry said. "Once the killer realises that Thea's disappeared, he might come after you, pile the pressure on so you tell him where she is." Harry paused, watching Thea's expression. She looked alarmed. "I also think Thea might appreciate having you with her. She's scared and needs her dad. I intend to place you both in a safe house where there's no possibility of the killer finding you."

"I'm still concerned about my work," Rob Connor said. "I'm up to my ears in cases that need my attention."

"Can't be helped. Get your admin assistant to lock up and go home, but don't tell them why. Make sure they know not to return until you say so."

"Can I get some stuff from the house?"

"No. You mustn't go back there. You'll leave directly from here. We'll send someone to get what you need." He paused for a moment — the girl had met the killer and that could be useful. "Before we finish, if I arrange it now, do you think you'd be able to help us create a photofit of the killer, Thea?"

"Yes. His face is imprinted on my brain." She shivered. "And there's something else. He didn't want to get caught on CCTV because he said the police would know him."

"When we get a good photofit, we'll see who recognises him. I'll sort that out and be back shortly." Harry looked at Thea. "You've done well. Later, we'll take you to the safe house and you can relax a bit. We'll speak again tomorrow when I've got more information from the laptop you gave me."

* * *

Harry returned to the main office to arrange a safe house for Thea and her dad. After a word with Rodders, it was agreed they would use a cottage on the outskirts of Stockfield, about ten miles from Ryebridge. It was up in the hills, out of the way but close enough for when Harry needed a word.

"Who'll you appoint as FLO?" Jess asked.

"This is so important that I hoped that you might take it on, Jessie." He saw the look. She wasn't impressed.

"But I should be working the case with you," she said. "We're close now, we need all of us on it."

"Thea's been so candid because she's terrified, but there's more to come. She knew Roebuck was about to be murdered, yet she did nothing. She stood by and allowed him to die just to suit her own ends. There's a side to that young woman I don't much like. She's utterly selfish and I don't trust her one bit. I'd like you with her in case she decides to make a run for it. And if and when she wants to talk again, you'll be there, on hand. You know what's important to us and what to disregard. Some other FLO wouldn't have a clue."

"I move into my new house on Friday, or have you forgotten? I have to be back in time for that."

"If needs be, I'll get a replacement then," he said, "but for the moment, a familiar face will keep Thea on side."

"You make sure you keep me informed about everything," she insisted. "No leaving me out of important breakthroughs. All right?"

"Absolutely. You're the one who updates the family, so no probs." He grinned. "Before you go, would you do something else? Take Col and nip round to the Connors' house and get them a few essentials."

Jess rolled her eyes. "You owe me, Harry Lennox."

CHAPTER THIRTY-SIX

He parked at the end of the leafy road where the Connors lived, and waited. It was late but the house was dark, silent. There'd been no movement. Not even the girl's dad, the solicitor, had returned home. Something was wrong — surely, he didn't work this late? Then he saw a car pull up and two people get out. Not the Connors, but he did recognise them both, they worked with the DI in charge of this case.

That could only mean one thing, the stupid girl had gone to the police.

The assassin hunkered down and watched the house in his wing mirror. It was vital they didn't see him. He was right, they had a key. That meant the police were protecting both Thea and her dad. That wasn't good. The girl could describe him. As for the evidence she reckoned she had, he would have to take the risk.

Fifteen minutes after they'd arrived the two detectives left, locking the front door behind them. Both were carrying suitcases — the Connors would no doubt be ensconced in a safe house, well out of his reach. He had to do something, get back control. The girl must be got rid of, and quick. But how? He smiled. Of course. There was a way. He knew exactly how to stop her. Thea Connor would not get the better of him.

It was simple. Follow the suitcases.

* * *

Harry rang Sasha at the Reid. "I don't have to tell you how urgent this is. We need everything you can find. Thea told us they used the buying-and-selling site we spoke about. Coded adverts. See what you can deduce. There'll be information on the laptop that should help."

"I'm looking at it now," she said. "The mobile was only used to call one number but it's no longer active."

"I think that's the killer's number, used exclusively by Calvert."

"You'll have to give me a bit longer with the laptop," Sasha said. "You'll be here tomorrow for Roebuck's PM, won't you? Pop in and I'll give you what I've got then."

"Thanks, Sasha."

Harry finished the call and saw Rodders standing at the incident board. "I've had Weeks on," Rodders said. "He wants everything we've got so far, particularly what we've gathered on Calvert."

"He's a bit eager. We don't know what we've got yet, Sasha is still working on it."

"Don't squeeze him out, Harry. We need the man onside. He gets a whiff that we're being cute and he'll take the lot from under our noses."

"We just need a bit longer, sir. Just so we can collate what we've got so far and piece it together. Currently we've got more on the assassin than Calvert, so the case is still very much in our hands. If Weeks snatches it from us now, it could jeopardise the case. We've just got an important witness on board. She's young, nervous, and it's us she trusts. Hand her over to the City boys and she'll clam up."

Rodders nodded and wandered off back to his office. Minutes later, the officer who'd done the photofit with Thea tapped on the door.

161

"What d'you think, sir?"

The image wasn't particularly good. It showed a clean-shaven, dark-haired man wearing a baseball cap and with the neck of his polo sweater pulled up over his chin. "It'll have to do. We'll get it circulated to the press, the local TV, although I'm not holding my breath on anyone coming forward."

Good or not, the photofit would rattle the killer, make him realise how close they were. And Thea was safe, which was reassuring.

CHAPTER THIRTY-SEVEN

Day Seven

First thing the following morning, Harry and Colin checked in with Melanie at the Reid. She'd already started the PM and had Roebuck on the table, his innards spread out across his lower belly.

"There were two stab wounds using the same knife," Melanie confirmed. "One struck his abdomen but didn't kill him. Roebuck was a big man, plenty of blubber." She grimaced. "The second wound penetrated the heart." She held the dripping organ aloft. "This kill is different from the others, not so clean. It didn't go to plan, the two men fought, and it got messy. Roebuck is bruised and cut about the face. It must have been quite a set to."

"It certainly was," Hettie chimed in. "That flat was in a right state — broken ornaments, overturned furniture, plus Roebuck was no housekeeper, so it's taken some sorting out. Still, we had one bit of luck." She held out what looked like a tiny, creamy-coloured stone. "One of my people found this lying on the carpet, and it doesn't belong to Roebuck. It's part of a tooth," she explained. "The tip of an adult canine to be precise."

"A what?"

"One of those two pointy ones near the front." She smiled. "With luck it'll belong to our killer."

"Roebuck punches him in the mouth and that happens," Harry said thoughtfully. "The killer must have noticed he'd lost half a tooth."

"It might not hurt but it'll feel wrong, sharp — if he hasn't looked in the mirror. It's worth checking with the local dentists, see if anyone has needed a front tooth fixing."

Harry made a mental note to speak to Hugh. He was a dentist, perhaps he could put the word out. "Can you get DNA from it?"

Hettie gave him a big grin. "Yep. And there's more. The cuts on Roebuck's face. I had hoped to get a trace of the killer's blood. There wasn't any, but there are tiny fibres in the wounds. I'm still doing some research, but it looks like they came from gloves — you know, those worn by your outdoorsy types who like all the gear when they go walking. If it's the ones I'm thinking of, they're expensive. They have full touchscreen compatibility so you can access your phone when you're out walking or running."

"They're usually leather, aren't they?" Harry said.

"So this guy likes to be different. Find the gloves and I'll match the fibres — and don't forget his boots while you're at it. I took a cast of a print that was found in the mud by the boating lake."

While Harry had been talking to Hettie, Melanie had continued with the PM. "This man was a walking time-bomb," she said. "Coronary arteries are badly furred. He could have had a heart attack at any moment."

That's as may be, but Roebuck had still been a force to reckon with. He was the only one of the killer's victims who'd tried to fight back.

"I'm doing a tox screen," Hettie said. "The whisky was laced with diazepam — that's a prescription drug. You'd have a job finding who it was prescribed to, and it might even have been bought online. If I get anything else that helps, I'll be in touch. But basically, where the rest is concerned, find me a suspect and I should be able to rule him in or out."

This good news lightened Harry's mood. "The blood on the grass — anything back on that?"

"Blimey. Give me chance," she chided. "But if it checks out with the sample of Isherwood's DNA, you'll be the first to know."

He left them to it and went to find Sasha. Not being permanent, she'd been put in the only space available, the basement. She'd done her best, turned the room into a makeshift lab and every surface was now covered in tech equipment.

"Made it your own, I see." Harry looked around, smiling. "Got anything?"

Sasha returned the smile. "I think I might have. I've had a look at Dean's third laptop. It was very informative. I found a hidden file where he'd described the code used to interpret the ads on that selling site. A sort of 'how to' guide on decoding them. Look, I'll show you."

She accessed the selling site and pointed to a particular advert.

"It appears to be a chest of drawers for sale, but it actually contains all the information the killer needs on the latest victim, Roebuck. The seller states that he's in Ryebridge. Now the killer knows where to find the target." She pointed to the object that was supposedly for sale. "This bit here is a name."

Harry was lost. "I don't see any name. All I see is a rather long and flowery description of a set of pine drawers."

"It needs to be that long to fit the whole code in. Dean's instructions say to go through the letters in the ad, taking some out according to the formula he'd worked out." Using the ad for the chest as an example, Sasha soon had the name 'Joe Roebuck' written on a scrap of paper. "It's simple really. Whoever places the ad just has to ensure that the words in the description fit the formula."

"Could be tricky."

"Hasn't been so far. I've found them all — Nadia, Lana, and a bloke killed a few months ago in Wilmslow. I'm still searching — there are some I haven't found. Your faceless man for instance, but given I don't know his real name, that's not surprising. The faceless man and the others were listed in advance in the ad, along with a number to call. I presume the man who hires the killer makes a quick call or sends a text using that phone Dean found, and the kill is on. All the killer needs to know is the number. No doubt he'll already have deciphered the ads and have the names."

It was a clever system. "It gives the killer time to do his research on the intended victims. One thing puzzles me, though," Harry said. "How does the killer know which ads to look at? There are hundreds on that site."

"The relevant ones are all placed by the same user." She pointed. "All the killer has to do is look for the username, 'Songbird'."

CHAPTER THIRTY-EIGHT

Songbird. This had to be a joke, one huge giving of the finger. Songbird was the name of the operation Weeks was running on Ricky Calvert. Harry needed an urgent word with Rodders, he must tell him what he knew about Weeks and his crew.

He drove back to the station. He missed Jess. He needed her take on this. One thing was certain, that username, Songbird, was no coincidence.

"Jess rang in about an hour ago," the desk sergeant told him. "She could do with a word."

"Likewise, but I've got to speak to Rodders first." He hurried along the corridor to the super's office and knocked on the door.

"Got any news, Harry?" Rodders said at once. "I've had City on again — that man Parkinson, asking for a report."

"We have made a breakthrough, sir. We now know how Calvert contacted the killer." He had to keep this simple, Rodders wasn't particularly tech savvy. "They used one of those buy-and-sell sites on the internet. Setting up an account is easy and folk trade under usernames in the main." He paused, wondering how he'd take the next bit. "Guess what Calvert's username is?"

Rodders held up a hand. "Sorry, Harry, this isn't my area. Computers give me a headache. I don't like the bloody things, never mind buying-and-selling on them. If I want to get rid of stuff, an ad in the good old local paper does for me. And as for those book-reading things—"

"Songbird," Harry said.

That stopped Rodders in his tracks. "What?"

"That's Calvert's username on the site," Harry explained. "He's bloody laughing at us!"

"I wonder if Weeks knows," said Rodders.

Harry shrugged. "Well, Weeks has been at this a while."

"You're thinking a leak, that someone at City is on Calvert's payroll?"

"I can't see any other explanation, sir."

"I'll have to tell Weeks, get his take on this. We don't know enough about his team to give an opinion," Rodders said.

"Bloody Parkinson," Harry said straight off. "I'll stake my pension on it."

"Better not, lad, you could be mistaken. In the meantime, we'll keep important stuff to ourselves, limit what we tell Weeks. We don't want Calvert finding out what we know."

"I agree, sir. And we should hold back from putting stuff on the system until you've had that word."

Rodders nodded, much to Harry's relief. His support on this would be important if Weeks started putting the pressure on about results.

Harry went back to the main office and rang Jess. "How's it going? Col dropped the stuff off?"

"Yes, and then he was off home. Said he was meeting Hugh in the pub for a bite to eat, lucky sod. I'm stuck out here in the middle of nowhere with a man who wants to be anywhere but here, a sulky teen and two officers who are lost without their uniforms. Casual they were told. One of them is in a suit, complete with tie for goodness sake."

"We've got a problem," Harry said, ignoring her prattle. "Sasha cracked the code for the selling site. She knows Calvert's username. Guess what it is — go on."

"I'm not up to playing games, Harry. I'm too tired."

"Songbird." He heard Jess catch her breath. "Calvert knows about the operation and I dread to think what else. He has to, it's the only explanation."

"Tread carefully, Harry. Don't go getting into something you can't get out of."

* * *

The killer followed the detectives' car to Stockfield and a detached cottage on a quiet lane. The location was perfect — what bothered him was the number of people around. The girl, her father, the woman detective and two other officers in plain clothes. It was seven at night, the house was lit up and he could make out people moving around inside. He'd have to strike in the early hours and be very careful about it. He'd get one chance at this. There might be collateral damage but whatever happened, the girl must die.

He decided to return to Ryebridge to think it through. He was about to set off when he received a text on his burner phone. It was Calvert. He said to forget Lana, Calvert would deal with her another way. He had a new job for him and had already placed the ad on the site. This time the fee was twice as much as usual. The target was high priority and needed to be taken out pronto. The killer was warned not to fail, he'd been getting sloppy of late. A warning? Sounded like it, and he knew what that meant. His usefulness was wearing thin. Calvert was losing trust.

He'd kill the girl, do the new job and move on. Ryebridge and the surrounding area was becoming too dangerous. Thea Connor had all the information Dean had gathered on him, and the police weren't stupid. It was only a matter of time before someone pointed the finger at either him or Calvert.

As he drove, the killer considered his options. London, he decided. He had contacts there. One man in particular, who had money laundering down to a fine art, would hire him in a heartbeat.

He was back home within twenty minutes. He planned to have a bite to eat, formulate a plan and then ready himself for the night ahead. He walked towards the door, reading the text again. The pay-off for the new job would be big — twice the usual fee was a huge amount. The target must be someone special, not that that bothered him. He slid the back off the phone, removed the sim card and dropped it down a drainage grill.

CHAPTER THIRTY-NINE

Jess never slept well on her first night in a strange bed and at two in the morning, she was still struggling. She'd be a wreck tomorrow and have to get by on strong coffee. Still, there wasn't much to do here — watching Thea was about it. The killer didn't know where she was, so how hard could it be?

Jess wasn't used to the countryside. Everything was deathly quiet, the only sounds were the rustle of branches in the wind and the odd hoot of an owl. As she lay trying to sleep, she went over the conversation with Harry again in her head. Weeks must have a dodgy officer, and Calvert was making a joke of all their hard work. He obviously felt safe, secure in the knowledge that no one could discover what was going on. But he didn't know how much information Dean had collected.

She might have dropped off but a loud creaking broke the silence and had her on alert. It must be someone on the stairs, off to the kitchen to get a drink. This was an old cottage, creaky floorboards were to be expected. The owl hooted again, making her jump. Jess decided that life in the countryside definitely wouldn't suit her. This was no use. Cutting her losses, she got up, intending to go down to the kitchen and join whoever was there in a pot of tea.

But downstairs everything was in darkness, the kitchen empty. The blinds were open, allowing the moonlight to stream in. The back garden looked weird, full of grotesque shapes and menacing shadows. Jess shuddered. She wasn't enjoying this. Suddenly the kitchen door slammed shut and she heard the key turn in the lock. Someone had just locked her in.

Jess went across and tugged on the handle, but it was no use. She had no mobile with her either, it was lying on the cabinet next to her bed. But she had to alert the others, Thea's life could depend on it. Jess had no idea how he'd found them, but this had to be the killer.

Think, girl, think. There has to be a way. Noise. Wake them all up, hopefully before he finds Thea. Jess grabbed a broom that was standing in a corner, stood on a chair and banged hard on the ceiling. The two officers were in the room above, they had to hear her.

Next came a series of loud thumps. Someone falling down the stairs? Jess screamed out, "I'm in the kitchen! Let me out."

"Sorry, Jess, he got away." One of the officers opened the door. "He fell down the stairs and legged it through the front door. But I think he's hurt. He fell awkwardly on his ankle."

"Get out there, he might still be hanging around." Jess ran up the stairs to check on Thea and her dad. Both were fine, locked in their rooms.

"It's okay," Jess said. "I don't know what happened, but it's sorted now."

Rob Connor wasn't convinced. "Was that him — the bastard who wants to kill my girl?"

"We can't be sure. The cottage has been empty for a while. Perhaps it was someone who's been using it to sleep in."

"You don't believe that any more than I do," he said sourly. "Get us somewhere else. This place is compromised. Somehow he's found out where we are."

He was right. They'd have to move them straight away. This was turning into a nightmare.

* * *

Damn that bloody detective! He should have torched the place, made sure that no one walked out of there. Now they'd move her again and Thea Connor would be lost to him. He needed to think. For the first time in his killing career he'd lost control and now he was in danger of becoming a target himself. All because of two meddling teenagers. If the man he worked for got a whiff of this, it'd be curtains.

Hang on. Why bother with Thea Connor? She wasn't a paid target. He could walk away, get on with the job in hand and earn himself a packet. As for Thea, he'd just have to play it close and hope the police didn't come after him. Why should they anyway? No one knew his true identity, not even her. In many respects he was as safe as he'd ever been.

He arrived home in the early hours. He'd fallen heavily down that narrow staircase and twisted his ankle. He'd need to rest up, spend the next few days researching his new target. All he wanted now was to do the job, get paid and get the hell out of Ryebridge.

He sat down at his laptop and accessed the selling site. Ah, good, his next target was local, no travelling. The hit list just gave him as 'faceless man', but after ten minutes on the ad Songbird had placed, he had a name. It sent a shiver down his spine. At first, he thought it had to be a mistake. But in his heart of hearts he knew it wasn't. It was his reward for having failed with the Midani girl. He'd also created too much publicity when he'd murdered Dean and that PA at the hotel. But what else could he have done? They had both been a threat to his anonymity. He recalled his conversation with Thea — she'd predicted this very thing. Clever girl. Perhaps he should have paid her after all. He looked again at the name he'd been given. He'd have to leave, and there was no time to lose.

CHAPTER FORTY

Day Eight

The following morning Harry was at his desk before eight. Jess had rung him about the break-in in the early hours, and he was worried about her. They were lucky it had ended the way it had. If Jess hadn't been awake and on the ball, things could have turned out very differently. A new safe house was swiftly sorted, and now even he didn't know where they were.

He had a batch of new emails, there were two from Sasha Steele. He opened the first. The blood on the grass he'd collected from the embankment near the bowling club was a match for Isherwood. The man had been telling the truth — he had got his bruises and scratched face from the tumble and not from a fight with Roebuck. It looked less and less likely that he was their man.

Colin arrived next, and he didn't look happy. "I've been thinking about Jess and the break-in at the cottage. I reckon it was my fault. I think we were followed. It's the only way the killer could have known where they were. He was probably staking out the Connor house and saw us collect their stuff. The suitcases were a giveaway. He must have guessed what was going on and taken it from there."

He could be right. "See if you can spot anything on the CCTV along the road to Stockfield. That's a good call, Col." He smiled. "Enjoy your night out with Hugh?"

He didn't look any happier. "He called it off, had to work. They had a burst pipe at his surgery, and he spent the evening mopping up."

Somehow Harry didn't see the suave Hugh Devereaux getting to grips with a mop and bucket.

Harry's desk phone rang, it was Rodders. "Would you come to my office? I've got DCI Weeks with me and he'd like a word."

This was it. How would Weeks take their theory about a leak on his team?

The answer to Harry's question was not well. Weeks hadn't liked what Rodders had told him one bit, and by the time Harry got to the office his face was one huge thundercloud.

"Before you start, Superintendent Croft has filled me in and what you say isn't possible. My team is tight, all hand-picked, so you can forget this wild idea of yours, Lennox."

"You've seen the website in question, sir? So how d'you explain it? How come Calvert takes the username 'Songbird' when he places his adverts? You're saying it's a coincidence that he uses the same name as your so-called covert operation?" Harry was angry too. Why couldn't Weeks see what was staring him in the face?

"No, I'm saying he's heard the word somewhere. Perhaps from one of yours."

Harry shook his head. "Out of the question. We've only been aware of Songbird for a few days. Before that it meant nothing apart from a brief mention in the odd email. Think again, sir. There has to be a leak and it has to come from your team."

"DI Lennox has a point," Rodders said. "Knowing the name of your operation is one thing but we have to consider what other information he's being fed. Right now we're hoping to have enough evidence to put Calvert in the frame for hiring the killer and the last thing we want is for him to get wind of that."

Weeks sighed heavily. "You can say that again. I've been after the bastard for too long as it is."

"Then help us, sir," Harry said. "Can I suggest that we keep all new information between ourselves? We have acquired a mobile phone that Calvert used to call the killer. It is being analysed by our forensic people. It will have fingerprints on it, possibly Calvert's DNA."

"Where did it come from?" Weeks asked.

"Calvert's desk drawer. Dean Greenwood took it."

"Not good enough. If it was stolen, it may be inadmissible. We need evidence got via a search warrant to make it work."

Harry felt deflated. That mobile was important to the case. "I'll speak to Sasha Steele, she's in IT forensics, see what she can turn up."

"It'll have to be good, and soon."

Harry was well aware of that. He'd no intention of reminding Weeks, but the killer had almost finished with all the names on Dean's board. Lana was still outstanding, but what was the chance of the killer finding her? That just left the faceless man. What plans, Harry wondered, did the killer have once he'd finished?

"Have you never suspected anyone in your team, sir? Anyone at all?"

Weeks gave Harry a long, hard look, as if to say he'd overstepped the mark. "I lead the team, with Parkinson as my second in command. We all have the same objective, to find something on Ricky Calvert that puts him away for a long time. None of my team would let me down. I've known and worked with them all long enough to be absolutely sure of that."

Harry still wasn't convinced but persuading Weeks would be a marathon. He'd have to let it drop for now. Meanwhile, as soon as he could swing it, he'd get a warrant to have Parkinson's bank accounts checked. All he needed was a good enough reason.

CHAPTER FORTY-ONE

What Weeks had said about the burner phone being dodgy evidence for convicting Calvert bothered Harry. But should it? He wanted sound evidence about the assassin, Calvert was Weeks's problem. He sat at his desk and read through the reports they had so far. In all of it, page after page, there was still nothing that gave the smallest clue as to who he was. The man was as much a mystery today as when he and Jess had first looked at Dean's wall.

Harry went back to his emails and opened the second one from Sasha. She'd found something else in Calvert's browsing history. He'd visited the Borders Holiday Park site. Dean had been there too. That couldn't be a coincidence. Sasha reckoned that Dean had been keeping an eye on Calvert's internet usage, had seen an ad on the selling site and deduced that the park would be the next location for a kill. The two men killed in Galashiels were connected to Calvert and not to a Scottish villain at all. What a relief! Harry cheered up immediately. This case was a Salton-free zone, which suited him just fine.

Harry decided he'd visit Maggie Greenwood and get more details about that holiday. While he was there, he'd speak to Isherwood, if he was home.

"Col, hold the fort, will you? I won't be long."

"Off anywhere interesting?"

"Another word with Maggie and to tell Isherwood he's off the hook. After that, I'll call in at the Reid, see if they have anything."

"I'll take a closer look at those photos shortly, you never know."

Maggie Greenwood seemed pleased to see him for once, and invited him in. "Making progress? Only you will tell me, won't you, if you arrest someone for what happened to Dean?"

"I will, and we are making some progress, but we still have gaps."

"Like who this bloody killer is," Isherwood chipped in from the lounge. He was sitting on the sofa and scowled at Harry when he entered the room.

"It all takes time," Harry said. "And this one is at the top of his game. I'm glad you're here, Mr Isherwood, I wanted a word."

"What d'you think I've done now?"

"Nothing, you're in the clear. Everything you've told me checks out, so I'm sorry if I had you rattled."

Isherwood grunted. "That's something at least. Glad you've seen the light."

Harry sat down. "I want to know whose idea it was to visit the holiday park in Galashiels."

"Mine, I think," Maggie said.

"No. It was Dean. He found the place online, remember?" Isherwood said. "He printed out the details and showed us one night. He was so enthusiastic that none of us could say no."

Maggie nodded. "I remember now. Yes, you're right. It was down to Dean."

Sasha was correct. Dean had been on the killer's trail even back then. "Can I have another look at his bedroom?"

"Why?" Maggie asked. "Your forensic people have been all over it twice already."

"Don't argue with the man," Isherwood said. "Up you go. Poke about wherever you want."

Harry climbed the stairs and went into the lad's bedroom. It had changed since he was last here. The wall with the faces on it was empty — forensics had taken all the images down and he now had them on his incident board. The tech was gone too, Sasha had that. Maggie was right, there wasn't much to see. The bed was made, the surfaces all clear and tidy. He opened the wardrobe and ran a hand over the clothes hanging there. Forensics would have gone through the pockets and the like. Harry was just about to leave when he spotted it.

He wouldn't have given it a second thought, except for two things Thea had said. At the beginning of the investigation she said Dean had something that gave him an edge, and later when she'd admitted the truth about trying to blackmail the killer, she had said Dean used spy cameras that looked like air fresheners.

Harry reached up and took the object from the top of the wardrobe. Who'd ever give it a second glance? It was just some innocent-looking product to make the room smell nice. Except it wasn't. Harry knew exactly what it was. He was holding one of Dean's cameras. He checked the slot underneath the stand — the card was still there. This had to be the 'edge' Thea had spoken of. The something Dean had intended to use if things got tricky. Shame he never got the chance.

"Everything okay?" Maggie asked when he went back downstairs.

He held up the evidence bag. "May I take this?"

"Yes, but I don't know what use it'll be. It's been on top of that wardrobe for ages."

He smiled. "I'm hoping it'll be just what I'm looking for, Maggie."

Back in his car, Harry rang Sasha. She was back in her lab and sounded almost relieved to hear from him.

"Come to the Reid, we need to talk. This is urgent, Harry, so don't be long."

She sounded anxious. He wondered what she'd found.

CHAPTER FORTY-TWO

Harry's mobile rang just as he pulled into the Reid car park. It was Isla Stewart.

"I'm going home this morning," she said. "It's pointless hanging around if you won't talk to me. But don't think this is finished because I will be back. One way or another, I will prove you're a fake and then I'll tell the world who you really are."

Harry was sick of rowing over this. "Whatever you want, Isla, but just ask yourself, does it really matter?"

"Yes, it does to me," she retorted. "Paul Lennox and I were due to be married, we loved each other. I can't pretend he's dead if that's not true."

"He is dead, Isla so you're wasting your time, and mine too. I have to go. Take care. Go home, forget all about Paul and get on with your life."

Harry finished the call. It was sad, and if he could have made it different, he would. But where he came from, anyone called Lennox had a price on their head. If Salton decided that there'd been a mistake and the wrong twin had died in that fire, he'd come gunning for him. Cruel and upsetting as it was, Isla was better off without him.

He drew up outside the Reid and went down to the basement where Sasha had her lab.

"There's to be another kill," she told him. "In Ryebridge. This time it's our mystery, the faceless man, but now I have a name, so you need to warn him, have him watched, do something to prevent it."

Harry took the notebook she handed him, where she had written down what she had calculated from the ad on the site and, underneath it, the name.

"There's no mistake. The number against his name is the same as that of the faceless man."

Harry looked again. No mistake she'd said. "I don't understand. I know this man. He's a nice guy. What's he done to upset Calvert?"

"You know where he lives?"

Harry nodded. "Hugh Devereaux is my next-door neighbour."

"Well, that's handy." Sasha stood watching him thoughtfully. "This couldn't have anything to do with you, could it? A warning for instance? Have you been rumbled as part of the Songbird operation? Stepped on toes, you know, upset someone?"

"There's a leak, so it's possible. But why choose Hugh? It doesn't make any sense that I can think of. I'd better go and find him, arrange some protection."

"Good call. But you could think of this as an opportunity, use Hugh as bait to catch the killer." Sasha smiled.

"Too risky. The killer is smart. Hugh's life must come first. He's another one that may have to go into a safe house."

"At this rate you'll have half of Ryebridge hidden away. But think about it, Harry. When are you going to get another chance?"

She was right. At least he should have a word with Hugh. It might shed some light. Find out who he knew and what he'd been up to recently for starters. He changed the subject. "Have you figured a way to get evidence on Calvert yet?"

"He placed the ads online. Find the computer he used, we'll match up the IP addresses and then we'll have him."

She made it sound so simple. "Calvert did most of his work, legitimate and otherwise, from his office at the Commodore. Dean had access so that'll be where he copied his browser history from."

"There you are then. According to the history, the Border Holiday Park was accessed from the same computer as the selling site. I found nothing interesting in his emails. All you need now is a bloody good reason to get a search warrant."

Isla's call and this thing with Hugh had almost made Harry forget about his find. He handed her the spy camera. "I got this from Dean Greenwood's bedroom. It'd been overlooked in the search. There's a card, I'd like to know what's on it."

"I'll make it a priority. Now, go and see your neighbour. Warn him and ask if he's willing to help catch the killer. You never know, he might surprise you."

* * *

Harry pulled up outside the apartment block. Hugh's car was parked up. Good, he was still at home. He hurried up to their floor and banged on his door.

"Hugh!" he called out. "It's Harry. I need to speak to you."

Hugh Devereaux opened the door. "Hello, Harry. What's up? Why all the panic?"

Harry pushed inside past Hugh, closing the door behind him. The place was spick and span as usual, but there was a suitcase on the sofa. It looked like he was packing. "Going somewhere?"

"Yes, and I doubt I'll be coming back," Hugh said. "A job offer I'd be stupid to refuse. I'll take what I need and send for the rest once I'm settled."

"I'm not sure that's a good idea," Harry said. "I have reason to believe you're in danger. Your name has come up in our current investigations as a target for a killer we've been chasing. This killer is good, Hugh. He's after you and won't give up until you're dead."

Harry watched Hugh's face and waited for a reaction. He remained expressionless. Harry couldn't understand why he showed no emotion, no fear. Most people would be terrified, they'd immediately have any number of questions. "This is no joke, Hugh," he said. "I'm deadly serious. This killer could strike at any time."

Hugh looked directly at him and sighed. "I know. I've seen the advert on the site too and I'm aware of what it means. I appreciate your concern, Harry, but there is nothing you or I can do."

CHAPTER FORTY-THREE

Harry stared at Hugh, open-mouthed. How could he know about the site? Then he realised. Hugh had to be part of this whole thing. "I don't understand how you know about the website. How and why did you get involved with these people?"

"Come on, Harry, you're the detective. Surely you can work it out. I know all about the site and the killings because I'm the man you've been looking for so desperately." He flashed Harry one of his charming smiles. "No sense in denying it now. You've done the investigating, gathered the evidence and now you know the truth."

The words struck Harry like a blow from a sledgehammer. When Sasha had shown him Hugh's name on that notepad it had never occurred to him that his neighbour — bland, dentist Hugh — could have anything to do with the murders. How could it?

The hairs on the back of his neck were prickling.

Hugh was their assassin, and he'd been living right next door.

But Harry was still puzzled. Hugh didn't fit the picture of the killer he had in his head. The man was cultured, always exquisitely dressed, a quiet sort who ran his own business and worked hard. Somehow, Harry still couldn't see him killing people with such cold, calculating expertise.

"But you're a dentist, not a killer. Were you forced into this?" he asked, still wildly searching for a rational explanation.

Hugh smiled. "I'm no dentist, Harry, that's merely a cover. But it's a good one. If you check the records you'll find a Hugh Devereaux listed, trouble is, he's long dead. I took his name and his qualifications because for the time being it suited my purpose. I've assumed many names and many jobs but none of them are the true me. I'm an assassin, Harry, pure and simple and I wasn't forced, it's how I choose to earn a living."

Shocked at the admission, Harry gazed round the room, looking for some evidence of this chosen profession. He noticed the suitcase. "Why are you leaving?"

"As you pointed out, my name is on the site. I value my life, simple as that. I've outstayed my usefulness, and now the man who hired me wants my blood."

"He'll have to wait his turn," Harry said. "You've just admitted you're a murderer, Hugh. I intend to arrest you."

"I don't want to harm you, Harry, but if you persist with the policeman thing, I'll have no choice." He pointed to the door. "My advice is to leave now and keep our conversation to yourself until I'm gone."

Harry shook his head. "I can't do that. If you're in danger, come in, give us a statement and we can protect you. We'll put you somewhere safe."

Hugh gave a dry laugh. "Sure. Like Thea Connor."

"Why did you want to kill Thea? What is she to you?"

"A thorough pain in the neck to be honest. She tried to blackmail me. Can you believe that? A mere teenager with no experience and a half-arsed plan. But give the girl her due, she did tell me this would happen, that I'd fall out of favour and become the first target of the new killer."

"You won't get away." Harry nodded at the suitcase. "Half the Manchester force is looking for you."

"That famous, eh? I'd no idea. I'm flattered." He checked his watch. "Sorry, Harry, but I'll have to bring this to a close. I've got a train to catch. You do understand, don't you?"

"I can't let you do that, Hugh."

"With respect, you can't stop me. I'm the killer, remember, and you are no match for my blade."

He was right, of course.

"Shame it had to be you. I had hoped to keep you and Col out of it. But that's not possible now. Sorry, Harry, but you'll have to become another of my tidy-up kills. That's what's made this entire operation so difficult and caused my employer to think again about keeping me on. Too many people got in the way."

Anger roused Harry from his paralysis. "People like Dean and Julia Bolton, for example, eh? You killed them without a second thought. And this employer of yours, would that be Ricky Calvert?"

Hugh smiled. "I can't tell you that. I do regret killing Dean though. I liked him. But he wouldn't do as he was told. And Thea is such a resourceful young lady. She'll go far, provided she keeps her nerve. What have you done with her now, by the way?"

"She's where you won't find her again. Thea will give evidence, she's already given us a description and a photofit."

"I've seen it in the local rag." He rolled his eyes. "You need to have another word with that young lady. She's still playing games. We met as she said, but I was not wearing a hat or that ridiculous polo-neck sweater pulled up over my mouth. I'm also aware that she's known our username for that site a while now. Her and Dean were keeping tabs on the intended kills."

She'd not said anything to Harry. What was she playing at?

"What's your plan?" he asked.

Hugh shrugged. "Flee. As you say, Calvert wants me dead, and he employs only the best. My time is limited, so whatever you want to know, Harry, make it quick."

"How long have you been doing this?"

"For as long as I can recall. I like the work, it's highly paid but does have its dangers. I've found the best course of action is to run before someone takes me out first."

"Why is he using the same username and format for the ads? He must realise that you'd see yours and be on your guard."

Hugh dismissed this with another shrug. "He doesn't care. The people he employs are experts at what they do. They'll get the job done whether I know or not. I use a knife, but the next assassin might favour a gun. I walk out of here and I'm a target." Hugh was staring at him thoughtfully. "There is a way out of this for both of us. I really don't want to harm you, Harry. Stand aside, let me go and tell your colleagues I'd gone before you got here."

That was never going to happen. Harry had no reason to protect either Hugh or Calvert. "Sorry, Hugh, can't do that. Both you and Calvert are going down. Calvert brings drugs into the country from abroad. A team from the Manchester force are after him. Do a deal, tell them what you know, and they'll do what they can for you when it goes to court."

That made Hugh laugh. "That's not going to work. Believe me, you'll never get close to Calvert and it's not in my nature to come quietly."

"You won't get away, Hugh."

"You know nothing, Harry." Hugh closed the suitcase and zipped it up. "So this is it then, the end. Shame — you and Col were good fun at times, relieved the monotony of this god-forsaken town."

Harry backed towards the door. If Hugh was to get out of here, he'd have to make a run for it. But just as he reached out for the handle his mobile rang, breaking the tension.

"Give it to me," Hugh said. "Come on. Throw it over here."

Harry slid it across the wooden floor towards him. Hugh stamped on it, hard.

* * *

Colin was in the main office giving Brian Isherwood's photos another look. He wanted to satisfy himself that he hadn't missed something important during his previous quick run through. No, there was nothing, no images of anyone lurking in the background when Dean had photographed his family.

He was about to go and get something to eat when the phone on Harry's desk rang. He reached across and picked it up. It was the FLO who was looking after Lana Midani.

"She's done one," the officer said. "She must have sneaked off during the night. Her things have gone too."

Just what they needed. "Harry took her phone off her. Did she have any money?"

"I'm not sure. She had her make-up bag. The thing is huge, there could be anything in it, and she's taken my mobile."

"Chances are she's making for London, and home. I'll get people on it. Stay there for now in case she comes back."

So much for breakfast. Lana was in grave danger and they needed to find her quick. Colin rang the railway station nearest to the house she'd been placed in, and then texted them an image of her. From there, she would probably catch a train to Manchester Piccadilly and then get an intercity to London. If that was her plan, with any luck they wouldn't be too late to stop her. On the other hand, she'd taken the FLO's mobile, so she might ring her friend Dante, the hairdresser, and ask him to fetch her. Colin decided he'd cover the train angle first, then get someone in the office to contact Dante.

He should tell Harry. He called, heard his mobile ring out a couple of times and then nothing. Harry had shut down his call. Colin was surprised — he always answered his phone — then he grew anxious. Was Harry in trouble? Not about to take any chances, Colin rang comms and asked for an immediate GPS trace on Harry's mobile. They told him the phone was in the apartment block where they both lived.

Colin was tempted to leave it. Perhaps Harry had gone home to change, or to grab a bite to eat. Perhaps he'd left his phone at home — no, he wouldn't do that. Knowing it would bug him if he didn't find out for sure, Colin grabbed his keys and made for the car park.

CHAPTER FORTY-FOUR

Harry had to do something to take the heat out of the situation. He needed to buy time, try to make Hugh see sense and come in. "You said to ask if there was anything I needed to know," he said. "Well, there are a couple of things."

"Go on, ask away," Hugh said.

"Have you always worked for Calvert?"

"Heavens, no. I've worked all over the country, usually for high-profile villains who don't like to get their hands dirty. As a rule, when a job is done, or a run of killings ends, both sides walk away and I find someone else who needs my services. Organised crime might be the bane of your life, Harry, but it's a godsend in my line of work. A good reference is all that's needed." He winked at Harry.

"How did you get into this? A man like you, you could have done anything."

"Killing pays," Hugh said simply. "It gives me money and a certain freedom that I enjoy. I make no bones about it, the job suits me and I'm good at it."

"So, what now?" Harry asked. "Effectively, your current boss is sacking you. As far as I can see, he's set the dogs on you, scuppered your chances of finding new work."

"I'll survive. Perhaps I'll go abroad. Someone out there will need my services. I just have to find them."

"Meanwhile, you've got a shadow stalking you. Can you live like that, Hugh?"

Hugh's expression darkened, his eyes took on a menacing glint. "Better than being incarcerated in a stinking prison cell. I'd rather take my chances while I still can."

He checked the time on his watch. "Now, if that's all, I have to make tracks."

"Dean Greenwood," Harry said swiftly. "When did you first become aware of him?"

"Scotland. He'd persuaded his family that it was a good place to visit. We met up, and at first, he was just a friendly kid, he made no mention of knowing what I did for a living. He went on about how we both lived in Ryebridge and what a coincidence it was that we'd met."

"He planned it," Harry told him. "He knew what you were up to. He was a clever lad, was Dean."

"I know that now. The holiday was him trying to pump me for information. Not that it worked."

Hugh reached into a drawer and took out a wicked-looking blade. He placed it in the open suitcase. "I really do have to wrap this up, Harry. Pleasant as it is to chat, I've got things to do."

"D'you really think you're going to walk out of here free as a bird?"

"Yes, I do."

"I bet Calvert's on your tail even now. Are you willing to take that risk? You're a fool if you are."

Hugh's face clouded. "Go on then, give me an alternative."

"Give yourself up. Come to the station with me and we'll talk this through properly."

"There's nothing more to say." Hugh picked up the blade and stepped towards Harry, who began to back up.

With his back against the door, there was nowhere else for Harry to go. He caught sight of a small coffee table standing in the corner. Reaching out with his foot, Harry tipped it up and sent it tumbling to the floor.

* * *

Colin entered his flat, only to find it empty. He was stumped. According to the GPS signal on his phone, Harry should be here. He was about to return to the station when he heard a crash coming from the next-door flat. Something was wrong. Hugh never made noise.

"Hugh? Harry, is that you?" he called out, hammering on the adjoining wall. "I'm coming round."

Colin darted into the corridor and started banging on his neighbour's front door. "Let me in!" he shouted. "I have backup with me. We'll take the door out if needs be."

Suddenly the door was flung wide and Colin was face to face with Hugh Devereaux.

"Ah, it's you," he said calmly and leaned out to look up and down the corridor. "Come and join us. Things are just getting interesting."

Colin saw his boss standing at the other side of the room. "Harry? You okay?"

"No, I'm not. This idiot is our assassin," Harry said.

"That smacks of sour grapes, Harry. Don't call me an idiot, please. What I do takes a lot of skill," Hugh said.

Colin looked from one to the other of them. "*Hugh* is the killer? Are you sure?"

"Oh, he's sure all right." Hugh shoved Colin back against the wall. "Join your friend, and no sudden moves."

Colin heard the words, saw the blade in Hugh's hand, but he still struggled to believe it. "You can't get away with this," he said. "We know who you are now, so there's nowhere to hide."

"I've figured that one out, thanks. And, sad as it is, that's why you will both have to die."

Colin looked at Harry for confirmation.

Harry shrugged. "Nutcase."

"You need to learn some respect," Hugh said, holding the blade to Harry's neck. "You know how dangerous I am. The last thing you should do is upset me."

It was time for the self-defence training to surface. "Why not? It's what I'm good at, upsetting people." Harry grinned. "That's true, isn't it, Col?"

Hugh glanced at Colin. That brief moment was all Harry needed to grab hold of Hugh's arm. He twisted it up behind his back. "Get him, Col!" he screamed.

Colin lunged at Hugh, sending him to the floor. He straddled his body and delivered a hard punch to his jaw. But Hugh still had hold of the knife, and with one swift movement he brought it down hard on Colin's free arm.

Colin cried out in pain and rolled off him, his blood gushing over the floor. Before Hugh could get up, Harry stamped on his hand and took hold of the blade. With his free hand, he rescued his mobile. The screen was broken but it still worked. As Hugh screamed that his hand was broken, Harry called for backup and an ambulance.

Harry removed his tie and threw it Colin's way. "Hold your arm up and wrap this tight around it. Get one of those cushions and press hard on the wound. I reckon he struck an artery." He hauled Hugh to his knees and then floored him again with a kick to the belly. "You should have come in quietly when you had the chance."

Hugh said nothing, he was doubled up in pain. Before he had a chance to get his breath back, Harry kicked him again, this time in the head. "That's for stabbing Col. Handcuffs?" he asked his injured colleague.

"Inside jacket pocket."

"This is police brutality," Hugh said, spitting blood. "There are rules about violence against prisoners."

"No chance. You were trying to escape, and you assaulted an officer."

CHAPTER FORTY-FIVE

Hugh Devereaux was put in a cell to await interview and Harry went to tell Rodders about the arrest. Now that all the hullabaloo had calmed down, Harry finally had time to consider what had just happened. Never in a million years would he have pointed the finger at Hugh. The man simply didn't fit the profile.

"I was living next door to him all the time," he told Rodders. "I can't believe it. He was the perfect neighbour — no noise, no trouble. I'm still shocked. He wasn't shy about admitting who he was either. Once he knew I'd rumbled him, he told me straight away."

"What d'you want to do about Weeks?"

"We've got the assassin downstairs, but not Calvert. Before we involve Weeks, we need to question Hugh and get the whole story. We need evidence against Calvert, and he can give us that."

"Weeks won't like it," Rodders said.

"Is there any need for Weeks to know yet? We've got the assassin and that's what counts."

"And you're sure he's the right man?" Rodders asked.

"He's confessed, and we have evidence that will match up — the chip from his tooth, the boot print, and with luck we'll even find the gloves he wore when he fought with Roebuck."

Rodders still seemed hesitant. "Okay, you've got twenty-four hours and then we'll have to involve Manchester. Get a full statement from him, Harry."

Harry nodded, satisfied.

"And well done," Rodders said. "You got him. All that hard work paid off."

Harry wasn't about to contradict the super but it was really Dean and Sasha's work that had got them to this point.

"How's DC Vance by the way?" Rodders asked.

"He's still in hospital, sir. The knife struck his brachial artery, so he had to have surgery."

"Will he be in long?" Rodders asked.

"Not sure. I'll visit later, make sure he's okay."

"Give him my best. He saved your bacon, I believe." Rodders smiled.

"He did indeed, dived straight in and took him on. It was unlucky that the knife got him, Hugh was just striking out blindly."

"Let me know if you get anything new from the interview."

The first thing Harry did on returning to the main office was ring Jess.

"I need you back," he said. "There's been developments. I'll send a replacement to you now. Thea and her dad should be able to return home soon, though once the report's gone to the CPS, Thea will have to answer for her part in this."

"Does that mean you've got him? How?"

"Sasha worked it out from the code Dean formulated. The faceless man was Hugh, our neighbour. I went to warn him and found him getting ready to run. He knew he was next on Calvert's list and came clean."

"But why admit what he'd done? He could have bluffed it out," she said.

"We both knew he was involved, and I wanted to know how. He told me the truth. He didn't see it as risky, since he had no intention of letting me walk out of that flat alive. Turns out he's not so charming after all."

"Are you and Col okay?"

"Col's in hospital. We all got into a bit of a scuffle and he was stabbed in the arm, but he should be fine. I'll give you chapter and verse when you're back."

"Seems I can't leave the pair of you alone for a minute without you getting into trouble. Give me an hour." Chuckling, she ended the call.

He'd no sooner finished talking to Jess than his mobile rang. It was Sasha from the Reid.

"Want to see something interesting?" she said. "Believe me, it's worth getting down here to watch."

Harry had intended to go the hospital and check on Col, but he could do that later. In any case, there was every possibility that he was in surgery right now. "Something on that disk from the spy camera?" he asked.

"Yes. And it's just what you need."

CHAPTER FORTY-SIX

"There's hours of everyday comings and goings on that SD card," Sasha said, "mostly in Dean's office at the Commodore. At first I thought there was nothing of any use — but then I found this."

Dean must have placed the camera up on top of a cabinet, as it took in most of the office. It was dark outside, so it was late. Nadia Nasir came in carrying a box and locked the door behind her.

"There's no sound, but you can plainly see that she's upset," Sasha said.

Nadia was crying, in a right state. She tugged at Dean's arm and kept looking at Calvert's office next door. Dean shook his head and appeared to be calming her down. Nadia pointed to a cupboard, then made a grab for the handle. Dean pulled her away.

"Wonder what she's after — the drug delivery that went missing?" Harry said.

"Possibly. Now watch this."

Nadia opened the lid of the box she'd brought in. Inside were several blocks of what looked like heroin, each individually wrapped in plastic. Harry squinted at the image. The substance in those plastic packages was pale brown in colour. Had to be heroin.

Nadia removed three of the blocks, stuffed them into her coat pocket and closed the box. Just then Agnes Wright, the manager at the Commodore, walked in. Nadia stood back as the woman spoke to Dean and then picked up the box from his desk. She and Nadia exchanged a few words, Agnes put the box into her shopping bag and left.

"She took it!" Harry exclaimed. "But where does that leave Calvert?"

"Disappointing I know, but he's not on the video at all. You need to get me that computer from Calvert's desk so I can check the IP address. Also, I could do with a look at Dean's desk — it may still have traces of heroin on it."

They'd need a search warrant for that. Calvert would know Hugh was in custody and wouldn't want them finding anything to connect the two. "Even if we tackle Calvert, he'll deny it, blame Dean most likely."

"Your best bet is this Agnes Wright woman. She's obviously involved with the drugs. Get her to talk to you."

Sasha was right. He had a lot of questions for Agnes Wright. He left the Reid, picked up a uniformed PC from the station and drove to the Commodore hotel.

* * *

The reception area was busy. "Agnes Wright?" he asked the girl behind the desk.

"She's busy in her office this morning."

Harry wasn't up for an argument. He simply showed her his warrant card.

Within a few minutes, Agnes Wright bustled through. She wasn't looking pleased. "This had better be important, I've work to do."

"So have I," Harry said.

"Whatever it is, I can't help you."

"I think you can. I suggest we continue this down at the station, where we can do things properly."

Agnes Wright shook head. "You're wasting your time. I can't tell you what I don't know."

Harry escorted her to the car and sat her in the back with the PC.

"I want my solicitor," she said. "I'll give you his number and you can arrange it."

Fair enough. Whatever it took to get her talking.

In heavy traffic, the drive from the Commodore to Ryebridge station took nearly an hour. The long journey seemed to calm Agnes down. When they arrived, Harry left her in an interview room with the PC. She'd given him the number of a Manchester solicitor. It would take him at least an hour to get here, and that was provided he wasn't busy. Harry decided to go and get a statement from Hugh Devereaux.

CHAPTER FORTY-SEVEN

Hugh Devereaux was sitting with the duty solicitor. He looked pretty relaxed for someone about to be charged with committing multiple murders. He gave Harry a smile.

"Right, Hugh," Harry began. "Time you and I had a chat. Treating you all right, are we?"

"This place is a dump. The building is out of the last century and has heating to match, but then you work here so you know that. Do I have to use the solicitor you arranged?"

"No, we can get you your own, I just need his name." Harry said.

"I've never needed one before." Hugh grinned mischievously. "What about that man Connor? He's okay, so I've heard."

Harry remained straight-faced. "He's out of town, I'm afraid."

"Okay, I'm happy with this one then. It won't make any difference anyway."

"You mustn't feel you're not being properly represented, Hugh. I don't want any complaints."

"I'm not sure what you want from me, but I've already said I did it," Hugh said. "I'm sure you'll search my belongings. There's a notebook among my things in the packed suitcase. Gruesome, I know, but the names of the dead are all in there. There are some who'd say noting down my kills is risky, but I've always done it, ever since my first victim. Call it a compulsion, name and amount paid, that's what you'll find."

"You're confessing? Just like that? No persuasion needed? I'm surprised. I thought you'd fight me all the way. Have you discussed this with your solicitor?"

"No point," Hugh said. "I'm guilty and I don't doubt you'll have evidence. All you're short of is my DNA."

"True," Harry said. "Well, we also need the boots you wore when you killed Dean, and those expensive outdoor gloves. We're keen to match them with a boot print you left in the mud near the boating lake, and the gloves left fibres on Roebuck's hands."

"There's always something. Forensics are just too damn good these days. No CCTV though, I'm very careful on that front."

"You certainly put your all into your work, I'll give you that. Even took a beating to account for the bruises on your face. Going above and beyond that was."

Hugh laughed. "Ah, those lads. I gave them all a tenner and they jumped at the chance of thumping some posh bloke."

"Very clever. It worked too."

"DNA, you said. Where did you get that from?" Hugh sounded interested but detached, as if he were discussing some everyday problem.

"You had a fight with Roebuck. He punched your face and chipped a tooth. We found it."

"Very good. I still haven't had that fixed."

"Who was paying you?" Harry asked.

"You know the answer to that, Harry."

"I want you to tell me. Say his name for the tape, Hugh."

"Ricky Calvert." Hugh said nothing for a few moments. "You do realise that has just sealed my death warrant? I'll be dead before the day is up."

Harry put that down to Hugh being dramatic and dismissed it. "Unlikely. You'll be safely locked in a police cell."

"Oh, you don't know Calvert. He'll find a way."

Harry leaned forward in his chair. "Then give me something I can use against him."

"I know very little. I killed for him, that's all. I wasn't part of his other activities. I know he imports drugs, from Turkey mainly," Hugh said. "Once the shipments arrive in port, they're put in the van that delivers the clean linen for the hotels."

Harry already knew that much. Roebuck had been one of those drivers. "D'you have any names?"

"No. The only names I was interested in were the targets. What else Calvert got up to was none of my business."

"Something went wrong," Harry said. "A delivery went missing and that's what started this entire series of killings. The two in Scotland, they worked for Calvert. He must have suspected they were involved. He suspected that the girl, Nadia Nasir, had taken the delivery from the hotel and given it to her sister, Lana Midani. Roebuck botched the whole thing, that's why he had to go."

Hugh shrugged. "Calvert doesn't like mistakes. He cleans up quickly and thoroughly. You should look out for Ms Midani, he's bound to set the dogs on her, have another go. And then there's me. There's no way he'll let me live. I know too much."

Harry stared at him in disbelief. He seemed so cool. Did he feel nothing? "Don't you regret any of those murders?"

"Dean," Hugh said at once. "He was a clever lad and had a future ahead of him. I took that from him, for my own selfish reasons. He even went to see you lot, but foolishly you dismissed it all as some adolescent's fantasy."

"I know," Harry said. "I've got uniform searching for the report. So far no one's managed to find it."

"If you had listened, he might still be alive," Hugh said.

"Would you really have killed Thea?" Harry asked.

"Yes, without a second thought. Watch her, Harry. That girl lies. She wants only what's best for Thea, and sod everyone else."

"You'll most likely be moved soon," Harry said. "The Manchester City force are after Calvert and they'll want to talk to you. Have you ever heard of Operation Songbird? That's the name of the investigation into Calvert's activities, and yours."

Hugh looked amused. "Songbird is what Calvert calls himself, his username for when he places the ads. He's taking the piss. He's a clever man, Harry, a formidable enemy to have. He knows what's going on. And you know as well as I do that the only way that can happen is if there's a leak."

"Why did you move in next door to Col?"

"I was told to, Harry. I suspect he's being set up. Someone close to Calvert is trying to cover his tracks. Like I said, a leak."

CHAPTER FORTY-EIGHT

The solicitor Agnes Wright had requested arrived promptly and asked for some time with her prior to the interview. Harry watched them through the two-way window until he thought he'd given them long enough. He had stills from the video on Dean's spy camera printed out and ready. Her reaction to them would be interesting. He and a PC joined her and the solicitor in the interview room.

"I'll make this short, Agnes, it's getting late." He placed a photo on the table. It showed her holding the box containing the heroin. "What was in it?"

"I can't remember," she said. "It's just a box."

"It's a lot more than that, Agnes. The box contains heroin, packs of the stuff wrapped in clingfilm. I'd like you to tell me what you were doing with it."

"That box had old paperwork in it, for the shredder, that's all," she said.

Harry ignored this. "Were you aware that Nadia had helped herself to three of those packs before you entered the room?"

The woman's eyes narrowed. "Is that why she was killed?"

"I suspect so, and right now I don't hold out much hope for you either. Calvert doesn't like it when he loses stock." Her eyes darted around the room, looking anywhere but at him. "What did you do with the rest of the heroin, Agnes? Give it back to Calvert? What did he say when he realised the delivery was short?"

She glanced at the solicitor, who was writing in a notepad. He was from a large practice in town and expensive, but he wasn't doing Agnes any favours. He appeared to be totally uninterested.

"I'm waiting, Agnes. How did you explain it?" Harry said.

"I lied," she admitted. "I told him the entire delivery was missing. I knew very well what the Nasir girl had done, I saw her. That stuff is valuable. I asked myself why she should profit and not me. I shoulder a lot of the risk. I knew someone who'd pay me well, so I took a chance."

"You let Calvert believe that Nadia had taken the lot? Didn't you know he would kill her? Didn't you even warn the girl? Tell her the danger she was in?"

"I didn't think Calvert would go that far. I left it a day, thinking things would calm down. But Calvert was like a raging bull. I told the girl to run, that I'd cover for her, but Calvert got to her first. There was nothing I could do."

"We both know you're wrong, Agnes. You could have come to us. If you had, Nadia might still be alive. You know what sort of man Calvert is."

"Yes. I'm sorry, I should have at least tried. I've worked at the Commodore a long time, so I've seen how he operates. He brings drugs into the country, distributes them to his dealers and has whoever crosses him killed."

"D'you have any evidence of that, Agnes?" Harry asked.

"I've just told you, haven't I?"

"Your statement is useful but we need cast-iron evidence if we're to send him down. We want Calvert put away for a very long time, so we need more."

"He's secretive, clever," she said. He could see she was becoming upset. "There's very few at work who know about that side of his business. I've never seen anything in writing, or on his computer. He doesn't even keep a desk diary."

"How do the deliveries get here?" Harry asked.

"By ship, in a container, and then by road. I know that much. He gets the laundry van to pick up the stuff at a motorway café and truck stop on the M62. Last winter when we had all that snow, it got delayed. He was on the phone to the driver most of the day."

"Which driver was that?"

"Roebuck. He used to do the pick-ups."

"D'you know when the next delivery is scheduled?" Harry asked.

"Friday," Agnes said. "He's already told one of the security staff that he's to take Roebuck's place. The poor sod thinks he's collecting new bed linen."

Harry would give Weeks this information and let him deal with it. Calvert was his problem after all. "Does Calvert suspect that you had anything to do with the missing consignment, Agnes?"

"No. If he did, I'd be dead by now. He thinks Nadia took the lot."

"What have you done with it?" he asked.

"It's hidden at home."

"I want you to take time off until we get the proof we need to convict Calvert. First, I want to know exactly where on the M62 this café is and then a plainclothes officer will take you home. You'll give him the heroin and stay inside until you are contacted by an officer from Manchester."

Agnes nodded. She stood up, ready to leave.

"You do understand, Agnes, don't you? You must do as I've said."

"Will you keep watch on my house?" she said.

"Yes. We'll make sure you don't come to any harm. One more thing. What happens to the drugs when they arrive at the Commodore?"

"Calvert puts the delivery in a huge safe in his office. It's hidden inside a cupboard. If you didn't know, you'd never guess it was there."

Agnes and her solicitor left the room. She'd just given him their way in. Wait for Friday's delivery and then search his office. He needed to speak to Weeks.

CHAPTER FORTY-NINE

Day Nine

The following morning, Jess was back at her desk. She smiled up at Harry when he arrived. "Miss me?"

"And some. I didn't realise you were so useful."

She grinned. "Cheeky sod. I went to see Col last night, didn't see you there."

"I rang him instead. By the time I'd finished here I was knackered. Yesterday was full on and then some."

"I'll let you off then. Anyway, Col's doing okay and already getting bored. He wants to come back, but that's out of the question for a while." She gave Harry a long hard look. "He did ask if you were looking after the flat properly."

Harry pulled a face. The truth was, he'd not had a chance to do much tidying up and the place was a mess. "I'll have it back in shape for when he comes home, never worry."

Harry gave her a quick rundown of the previous twenty-four hours. "Weeks is going to watch for the delivery to be picked up on Friday and he'll follow the vehicle back to the Commodore. He'll have a search warrant ready and raid the place."

"What about our killer, your friend Hugh?"

"He's not my friend, and he's being transferred to Manchester today. Weeks wants to interview him, see if he can add anything to the body of evidence they've gathered on Calvert."

"You have been busy. I don't know. I turn my back and you solve the case. You're just after all the glory, aren't you?"

"If there's any glory going, I suspect it'll be Weeks and his team that get it. Operation Songbird belongs to them, we'll simply get a brief mention in a report no one reads."

"Not fair, is it? Weeks and his team sat on their arses while you worked yours off and Col got stabbed. Does that mean case over as far as we're concerned?"

"Looks like it. We took a killer off the street, Jessie, that's what matters. We should be pleased with ourselves. Who picks up the credit is secondary to keeping people safe. Speaking of which, I need a word with Hettie." He picked up the office phone and called the Reid. "Have you done a search of Devereaux's flat yet?"

"I've got a team on it now."

"There's a notebook, a list of the people he's killed. You'll find a metal box in the wardrobe — the key's hidden in a carton of juice in the fridge. It's another piece of evidence and it might help with the unsolved cases."

"Okay, Harry, I'll let you know when we've found it. He made a list of all his kills?" Jess shivered. "That's a bit much. Glad he's being shipped out this morning, and that I didn't have to deal with him after all."

There was a knock and DI Jack Parkinson poked his head around the office door. "So this is your little hidey hole. Can't the powers that be find you somewhere better? Bloody cold too, wouldn't do for me." He grinned.

"What d'you want?" Harry asked.

"I've come for your assassin," Parkinson announced cockily. "Get him back to Manchester and interrogate him properly."

"We got a full statement. There's a copy on the system."

"And very good it is, but there'll be more, there always is."

"Are you on your own?" Jess asked.

"I've got a driver waiting in the car park. Our man will be in handcuffs, of course. He's no danger, not anymore."

"Just don't lose him," Harry warned. "We worked hard getting this far and can do without the likes of you botching it up."

"Me? Botch it up? That's rich coming from you. One of yours snitched to the enemy, Harry. The assassin knew exactly where the safe house was, and then there's the name of the operation." He laughed. "But never worry, there'll be an investigation. Weeks will get to the bottom of it."

"Not one of ours, Parkinson. Look among your own people."

Parkinson was still laughing when he left the office.

"He's a piece of work," Harry said. "You know who he's pointing the finger at, don't you? Our Col. Just let him try to take it further."

"Calm down, it looked like he was joking to me."

"Parkinson doesn't do jokes. The man's a menace and a troublemaker."

CHAPTER FIFTY

Hugh Devereaux had passed an uncomfortable night on the narrow hard bed in his cell. He had spent the time trying to formulate an escape plan. He'd been told he was to be transferred to the Manchester station and knew this was his only chance.

He'd expected officers, to be caged in the back of a van without windows like a wild animal. What he got was Jack Parkinson. First mistake.

"You're not going to give me any trouble, are you, Hugh?" Parkinson whispered as they made their way down the corridor. "Mr Calvert wouldn't be pleased."

Hugh turned to look at his escort. He was grinning. This was a set-up. This officer was in Calvert's pocket — had to be. Hugh knew that unless he acted, he'd be dead before the journey was up. It was a case of Parkinson or him.

Parkinson sat with him in the back of an unmarked police car. Hugh wasn't even handcuffed. Second mistake. "I know what this is," Hugh said. "How d'you intend to pull it off? There's a uniformed officer at the wheel who can call for help within seconds."

"He won't. He's being paid well enough."

So that's how it was. He had to put a stop to this and quick. His mind was racing.

Leaving the car park, the driver ignored the signs for Manchester and instead turned towards the road that went over the hills.

"How are you going to do it?" Hugh asked.

"Thought I'd take a leaf out of your book and use a blade." Parkinson grinned. "This one, in fact." He took a wicked-looking knife from his pocket and dragged it lightly along the side of Hugh's neck. "In a minute we'll be turning into a country lane. Best get all your questions asked quick, because you won't have long once we're there."

Parkinson had put the knife back in his inside jacket pocket. This was his chance. Hugh leaned across him to look out of his window and nodded. The driver wasn't interested, he was one of Parkinson's men and had no doubt been told to turn a blind eye to whatever he saw or heard. "This is the back way to Stockfield. I know it well, I've walked all over these hills."

It was enough. Momentarily distracted, Parkinson relaxed his guard and turned to look at the scenery. One swift move and a split second later, Hugh had the blade out of Parkinson's pocket and in his hand. Another second and he pushed it hard into Parkinson's chest. He didn't even have time to scream. He simply slumped forward, the grunt that escaped his lips drowned out by the sound of Hugh loudly clearing his throat. The PC at the wheel, too intent on negotiating the twisting road, remained oblivious.

"Pull up," Hugh ordered.

"Mr Parkinson said not to stop until he says so, sir."

"He can't answer. Parkinson is dead, so I'm afraid you have no choice. Pull up, idiot, or I'll slit your throat."

* * *

So, Calvert had sent Parkinson to kill him. Hugh had to make this stop because there'd be others to follow. Calvert would become a persistent problem and not even he'd be able to outrun the man for ever. There was only one solution. He had to get to Calvert first.

The idea appealed to him. That man had dished out the orders for long enough, and although Hugh was handsomely paid for what he did, it was Calvert who'd ultimately made the fortune.

Now at the wheel of the unmarked police car and Parkinson's warrant card tucked in his pocket, Hugh headed for Manchester and the Commodore hotel. In all the time he'd worked for Calvert, he'd never met him face to face but he'd seen photos in the press. The man wouldn't be difficult to identify. Hugh was looking forward to this. Killing Calvert would wipe the slate clean, freeing him of the villain for once and for all. As for Parkinson and the PC — collateral damage. They worked for Calvert, had taken his money and knew the risks. The only problem where they were concerned was how long it would take their colleagues to find them.

The reception desk at the Commodore was busy. Hugh walked straight up to one of the girls behind the desk and asked for Calvert. She was about to tell him that wouldn't be possible when he flashed the warrant card at her. "I won't keep him long," Hugh said, smiling. He waited patiently while she rang Calvert's office.

"A DI Parkinson for you, sir." She listened. "You can go through. Along the corridor and first door on the right."

So far, so good. Calvert's office was at the front of the building overlooking the busy Oxford Road. Seated at his desk, Calvert didn't even look up as Hugh entered.

"I said no meetings. I hope for your sake you've done as I said, and this is now over."

"Almost," Hugh said. "Just a little tidying up to do."

Calvert's head shot up. "What the hell have you done with Parkinson?"

Hugh could see from the look on the Calvert's face that he'd guessed who he was. "Sadly, he's gone the way of so many others. Pity it couldn't have been different, but the man was hell-bent on killing me."

"What d'you want?" Calvert blustered. He was in his mid-fifties, heavy set with hair far too black for his age. Hugh smiled to himself. Poor bloke, clinging to his youth and failing miserably.

"Money," he said. "The contents of your safe will do, and you off my tail."

Calvert shook his head. "You've had all you're getting. You've had a fortune off me over the years." He waved at the door. "Now, get out of here."

"I don't like your tone," Hugh said, moving closer to him. He glanced towards the cupboard containing the safe. It was open, the safe door ajar. "Been counting your ill-gotten gains, have you, Ricky? You want to be careful who sees that."

"Get out before I have you thrown out. You and me are done."

"Not quite. You see, in my trade it doesn't do to leave loose ends."

Calvert never knew what hit him. Before he had time to draw another breath, Hugh had stabbed him through the heart. Job done, he cleaned out the safe and returned to the car.

EPILOGUE

"When are they letting you out?" Harry asked.

"They want to do more tests tomorrow," Col said. "Providing all's well, I'll be discharged the day after."

"In that case, I'd better tidy up the flat a bit."

"Harry, you've not trashed the place, have you? Please tell me it's as I left it."

Harry wished he could. He was sorry but the Songbird case had taken up the last few days, leaving him no time for anything else. Added to which, Calvert's murder had thrown everything into a spin. "It'll only take me an hour or so to sort it."

"I'll give him a hand," Jess offered.

Harry and Jess were eating fish and chips. Harry held out his package to Col. "Want some? Bet the food in here is crap."

"To be honest, I'm not hungry. My bloody arm aches and my sister Kate's been bending my ear ever since I came in here. What with her problems and him in the next bed's snoring, I was awake all last night."

"What's wrong with Kate?" Jess asked.

"She's left her bloke. It's his house, so she's been kipping on a mate's sofa. Basically, she needs somewhere to live."

Harry looked at Jess and then at Col. He knew what this meant. Goodbye shiny new flat and ordered life with Col and hello god knows what. But Col had to put his sister first, and it wouldn't be fair not to offer. "Look, I'll find somewhere else. I can be out of your hair by the weekend."

Col brightened immediately. "Are you sure? It would sort the problem if I could give her your room until she's settled."

"No worries, and I'll leave the place like a new pin." It wasn't a surprise. Harry had known cohabiting with his DC could only last for so long.

Jess nudged him. "Where will you go?" she whispered.

"A B&B somewhere, but let's not do this here. I don't want to make Col feel bad, he could do without the stress."

Jess smiled. "Tell you what. I move into my new place tomorrow. Help me move my stuff and you can have my spare room for a while."

Her offer was totally unexpected. "Really? I'm not dreaming, am I? You did just say that?"

Col grinned. "I heard her too. She must have taken to you at last."

"I won't forget this, Jessie. I owe you big style." Harry was genuinely grateful. "What about that girlfriend you wanted to move in?"

"Can't afford it, can she? But don't worry, I won't let you forget what I've done. I'll be charging rent too, so you'll be paying your way."

"Whatever you say."

Meanwhile, Jess was scrutinising her mobile. "She's got some nerve. Lana Midani is all over social media, telling the world what a narrow escape she had and how her friend Dante saved her life."

"I think she'll find it was us," Col said, helping himself to some of Harry's chips. "But now we know how she got back to London — she must have used the FLO's mobile and called him."

"And like a fool he did as he was told," Jess added. "Speaking of FLOs, what'll happen to Thea?"

"A file has gone to the CPS, so we'll have to wait and see," Harry said. "The same goes for Agnes Wright, who took a fortune in heroin and admitted she had plans to sell it."

"And all because of Ricky Calvert. Shame Weeks couldn't get him to trial. I bet he regrets that one," Jess added.

"Who knows? He'd have fought the case anyway, blamed everyone but himself."

"We did have evidence though," said Col. "The statements, for starters."

"True, and the IP addresses used to place adverts on that site. Sasha did a great job matching them up to Calvert's computer. But he'd got away with it before, so if the case had gone to court, who knows what might have happened."

"What about Devereaux, our assassin?" Jess asked. "Who's looking for him?"

"Us, Europol and various agencies in the States, but I doubt he'll be found," Harry said, offering the chips round.

"Who'd have thought Hugh could do such things? He seemed such a pleasant bloke," Col said. "Had me taken in completely."

"He had us all taken in, Col. He actually had the cheek to send me one last text, the day he killed Calvert. He said he was sorry it had ended this way and if I valued my life, I shouldn't look for him. That notebook of his had dozens of names listed. Manchester are checking through them, reckon it'll help put a lot of cases to bed. Stupid to keep a record like that, but I guess some sickos like to glory in their evil. No matter what the risk."

"Glad I never asked him to look at my teeth," Col smiled.

"He was no dentist. Hugh's identity all belonged to a dead man. But he looked the part, give him that. I can picture him in a white coat wielding a drill."

Harry saw Jess shudder. "He's a one-off that's for sure. A mystery man. Now gone into hiding, probably never to be found, but thankfully, not our problem anymore."

"Now I'm pleased I was saddled with looking after Thea," Jess said. "I still think of Hugh Devereaux as that blank face on Dean's wall. Well, he can stay that way. I'm just grateful I never actually met the faceless man."

THE END

Thank you for reading this book. If you enjoyed it please leave a review on Amazon or Goodreads.

We love to hear from our readers. If there is anything we missed or you have a question about then please get in touch: feedback@joffebooks.com

Join our mailing list to get new releases and great deals every week from one of the UK's leading independent publishers.

www.joffebooks.com

Manufactured by Amazon.ca
Bolton, ON